Keeping the lid on

Neil Thomas

THOROGOOD

Published by Thorogood
10-12 Rivington Street
London EC2A 3DU

Telephone: 020 7749 4748
Fax: 020 7729 6110
Email: info@thorogoodpublishing.co.uk
Web: www.thorogoodpublishing.co.uk

A CIP catalogue record for this book is available from the British Library.

ISBN paperback: 9781854188984
ISBN eBook: 9781854188991

Printed and bound in Great Britain by
Marston Book Services Ltd, Oxfordshire

PART ONE

1

THE SCHOOL HAD BEEN MANY things to many people and not just as a school. For a start, it had been the elegant country seat of a long-forgotten coal baron who elevated it from its Jacobean origins into a minor Victorian masterpiece.

Successive industrialists had extended it in every direction, most notably adding an extensive stabling block, built around a central courtyard and entered through an elegant archway with a clock-tower cupola over its top.

The ownership by a leading iron tycoon had left a legacy of ironwork around the estate in fencing off the house from the land and in constructing an intricate folly and other fanciful shelters dotted around the park. He had gone to town on the main building itself with its loggia and adjacent orangery to the rear.

The front entrance to the two-winged house was through a magnificent wrought-iron gate in the middle of a low wall, with railings on top, which joined the two wings. Then, it was straight ahead over the York stone paving to large double doors that gave onto a main hall that seemed to be made entirely of wood: wide oak floor boards, panelling, pillars, pilasters, posts, banisters, staircase, a huge carved wooden fire surround and a vaulted and hammer-beamed roof, to say nothing of the 'brown furniture' that inhabited the large space, seemingly at random.

The smell of wax polish was overwhelming and no one who entered could prevent it lingering long after they had left the building. Permeating everything, it was as if the house and its history were preserved in wax and begging to remain as found.

Before you got to the house itself, you had to go up a very, very long drive. A walled and, yes, iron-gated main entrance, with its obligatory adjacent single storey gatehouse, gave access to the drive which passed field after field of farmland before entering the School grounds proper.

Carefully prepared rugby pitches, cricket squares and a couple of pavilions lay on either side of the drive, which then went through a wooded area where various outbuildings (now full of groundskeeping equipment) and cottages (now used by key staff members as their homes) were dotted amongst the trees.

The drive went on for a little way, before opening out in front of the main house to an area where you could park your car.

Signs then displayed that you should leave the School by continuing on the drive past the house and on through an area where the School farm was located, then past the old estate church and on over a bridge across a river and, finally, to the lesser, but still ornate, iron back gates which marked the end of the School domain.

The drive, the grounds, the house, the outbuildings – the layout and the structures as well as the history of the place – all seemed to have been a preparation for its life as a school.

So typical was it, in fact, that it could have been chosen by some canny location finder as the setting for the school scenes in any production of a major film that needed to feature a minor public school.

As befits a stately home, it was hidden from the main road, but there were surrounding hills that offered a vantage point in such a film to a sinister figure who could use binoculars to locate and spy on, say, a new teacher with a dodgy past who was trying to lie low at a boarding school; a misfit, but, strangely, not out of place in the fictional school.

It was such a good example of a school of its kind that had Evelyn Waugh known of its existence, he would have used it as the setting for *Decline and Fall.*

Films like *Tom Brown's Schooldays, If. . .*, *The Awakening, Goodbye, Mr Chips* or *Dead Poets' Society* could all have been shot there.

2

It will take no great imagination, therefore, to visualise the School and its grounds as being a perfect film backdrop for a scene depicting the funeral of its Old Headmaster. Except, of course, it was happening for real.

It has to be remembered that the original Founder of the School was an ex-military man who, sometime before, on leaving the armed forces, had seen the commercial potential of running a public school. There was, therefore, a military streak running through the place: parents found that comforting – they could trust military types to turn out self-reliant young adults.

And with the military involved, there was surely nothing that could happen that would faze them, so your child would be safe at all times. After all, if you are to abandon childcare and the safeguarding of your offspring to third parties, you would want those in charge to have some sort of track record in discipline, order, leadership and logistics, wouldn't you?

So, it was typical that, on the day of the funeral, the drive, all the way from the playing fields to the wooded area, was lined on both sides – and at intervals of ten feet precisely – by all of the School's pupils, a few hundred of them, in uniform, with their heads slightly bowed and their hands behind their backs. The funeral cortège made its way slowly to the church for the packed funeral service and the Old Headmaster was 'dispatched' with all due ceremony.

3

THE FOUNDER WROTE ALL THE parents a fitting letter, praising the achievements of the Old Headmaster, but focusing on the future of the School. After all, he had fee-paying parents to consider and the ongoing care and education of their precious children to address.

And so, he was…

…absolutely delighted that the Deputy Head will be taking over as Acting Head until a thorough and rigorous process is completed and a permanent appointment made.

In the meantime, parents can be assured that the School will continue as normal, maintaining its high standards of child welfare and learning that are so very well established as to be an intrinsic element of the very fabric of the School.

The Acting Head is well known to all parents and pupils, particularly those members of the senior rugby squad and all those who take a serious interest in cricket, as well as to those who value his amusing explanations of intricate maths problems.

And who can forget his witty speech at the annual Summer Ball (which, I can report, raised £2,067.68 for the pavilion match-day sandwich tables), made when deputising for the Old Headmaster who had sadly been taken ill only that very morning!

You can rest easy in the knowledge that the School will go from strength to strength based, as it is, on its strong foundations. That will be the legacy of the Old Headmaster. The flag of achievement was run up the pole by him and it continues to fly there still.

The letter was well received by all the 'sporty' kids' parents, who knew the Deputy Head well and had enjoyed post-match hospitality and banter with him. They had read the letter and, reassured that there was to be no immediate regime change, had casually tossed the letter into the nearest wastepaper basket.

The 'non-sporty' kids' parents, who found him rather boorish and awkward, read the letter a couple of times rather intently and then, grimly, filed it away.

4

BEHIND THE SCENES, THERE WERE, perhaps naturally enough, some concerns about the future of the School. The Old Headmaster had pioneered various initiatives that had translated directly into increased fees and reduced costs.

For example, not only had he led the way in accepting those with learning difficulties (both the trendy newer ones and the older, more traditional varieties), but he had dispensed with expensive catering – taking, as he colourfully put it, a 'bums and tums' approach – getting bums on seats and reducing the cost of feeding their owners.

The Old Headmaster had also embraced the overseas student market, regularly travelling to the Emirates, the Far East and oil-rich Nigeria on recruitment drives, as well as tapping into the subsidised armed forces of the UK and Commonwealth countries as a source of pupil recruits.

The main question posed in the staffroom was how on earth the Acting Head would be able to continue as commercial as well as academic leader of what was now a sizeable operation that had the welfare of so many staff and pupils at stake.

The relationship between the Founder and the Old Headmaster had worked well; both were ex-forces – one hearty and one arty – and that combination had played well in the development and success of the School.

They had had one go at what they had read is called 'succession planning', but that had ended in disaster. They had selected a very smooth deputy head from a different school and well out of the immediate area. Of course, this had put many noses out of joint on the staff and amongst the parents.

Senior staff had been overlooked in making that appointment and parent favourites had clearly been rejected. A frenzied PTA campaign had started to undermine the new deputy head and promote the cause of their candidate. An unruly annual meeting had seen parents tabling motions of no confidence and trying to appeal to parents at large to threaten to withdraw pupils to 'hit the School where it hurts'.

The Founder and Old Headmaster had tearfully called for calm and, appealing directly to those parents who hated the PTA, asked for time to bed in the new deputy head.

The agitators got their way, in more ways than seventeen, because within a few weeks the new deputy head – sensing he was on a hiding to nothing – had run off with a recently appointed young matron, leaving only a note that they had 'gone South'.

So, perforce, the previously overlooked maths and games teacher (and parental favourite) was appointed as the deputy head. Now, as a surprisingly unforeseen consequence of the death of the Old Headmaster, he had become Acting Head. The agitators had got what they had wished for. They had not been careful in that.

5

IT WAS AT REGULAR MEETINGS of the owners of the School that financial matters were discussed. Most parents thought that, in some way, the School was a charitable organisation only interested in making a profit so that the facilities could be maintained or even improved. That was what the PTA thought too: let's raise funds for the School so that it can save its resources for major developments.

The owners knew different: that a well-run school can be a commercial goldmine, its educational status masking its moneymaking potential. Of course, the Founder had always been careful to refer to any 'profit' as a 'surplus' – 'an altogether less vulgar term', as he put it.

He and the Old Headmaster could celebrate a 'surplus' quite openly – the same as farmers saying that they've had a 'bumper harvest' when what they mean is that they have had a cracking year and have made shed-loads of money. And you can still pay handsome dividends out of a surplus, and guilt-free too! That was only taking the cream off the top after all.

The new Acting Head had, on paper, a good academic grasp – an adequate degree and even a teaching qualification. Hey, it didn't matter that he didn't have a higher degree did it, with so many years' teaching experience under his belt? He was well up on government and private school rules, regulations, systems and methods. Surely his commercial and business side could be worked on to good effect?

It was at one these owners' meetings after the death of the Old Headmaster that the Bursar had anxiously pointed out that the pupil roll was declining and his projections were for a loss for the first time since he had taken over the School finances twenty years earlier.

He had, naturally enough, been in a proper regiment, just like the Founder and the Old Headmaster, and his experience at handling his Mess accounts had made him a shoo-in for the job as Bursar when the School started expanding rapidly.

Always smartly turned out in his all-weather tweed suits, with his hair and moustache as neatly kept as his financial ledgers, the ever-dependable Bursar presented a very reassuring front.

He was totally unable to contemplate a deficit. Balancing the books was all that mattered and he would have court-martialled himself if he had been out of balance on either the debit or the credit side of things.

Straight after announcing the forecast loss, he offered to fall on his sword, but was persuaded to hang on until things were straightened out.

The Old Matron, who had a few shares in the School and had been around since the year dot, had long doubted that the Acting Head was up to the job. She happily voiced what she said was the Old Headmaster's generally low opinion of him, not just of his people skills and his financial awareness, but as 'someone who needed to be kept an eye on', whatever that meant.

The Founder gazed long and hard at the soft-edged features of the Bursar, then met the face of the no-nonsense Old Matron.

I am going to have to do something about this committee and pretty quick, he thought, but instead told them that he took their worries on board and would think about what to do next.

What he actually thought later was, If they think I'm going to go through a lengthy recruitment process and pay out a fortune in headhunter's fees, they've got another think coming.

If he was really honest with himself, the Founder was feeling very comfortable with the Acting Head and he was beginning to wonder why that was. Could it be as simple as the fact that both he and the Acting Head had been to minor public schools themselves?

The Old Headmaster had been a grammar school boy who had, admittedly, done exceptionally well – largely by his own efforts – and had won a commission into the army, passing out top in his officer training. He had turned out to be a first-class headmaster.

But there was something in his simple desire to turn out pupils who were genuinely happy and fulfilled that didn't seem quite right to the Founder. Maybe that mission came from his grammar school education?

In contrast with this approach, the Acting Head seemed, instinctively, to believe, as the Founder himself did, that a public school should turn out pupils who could keep their feelings hidden. It was more important that they should turn out well-rounded children who could conform than worry that anyone else should be aware whether they were happy or sad. That approach had got *him* through life all right.

That was why he had never understood why the Old Headmaster had got so worked up when Shirley Williams and her gang did away with grammar schools. Dash it all, could he not accept that he was now at a public school himself, which is really a comprehensive school when all is said and done – even if it is a fee-paying one.

Sure, they had entrance exams, but that was only to give the semblance of selection and help in the admittedly random award of scholarships and bursaries: poor results – give them an all-rounder scholarship; dire results – give them a sports scholarship; children from large families – give them a bursary to encourage them to send their other children. Surely the Old Headmaster could see that they were inclusive just like a comprehensive in fact and, surely, he should support comprehensives?

The Old Headmaster had loosely banged on about 'grammar schools breaking down class barriers', as if being well-educated really mattered to one's status in life! Huh!

At least he didn't get all that guff from the Acting Head and, say what you like, it had said in the reference they received from his previous school that 'nobody has a bond with the boys quite like his'.

6

The Bursar felt better having come clean about the figures, but it didn't stop him feeling slightly ill every lunchtime when he emerged from the staff dining room and knew he had to go back to his office.

Had he eaten too much or too quickly, or was he queasily uneasy about digesting the implications? How could he get rid of the anxiety?

He decided he needed to start going for a stroll in the grounds after lunch. That would calm his nerves in a situation like this and stop him obsessing about the School going bust and his pension going west.

His new regime had yet to start working. He was still sleeping fitfully, having the strangest of dreams and aware of every noise inside and outside of the bedroom he shared with his wife of forty-plus years. Some of his dreams were incomprehensible, featuring almost blind panic at him not having done enough work to pass his officer training exams all those years ago, which he had in fact passed with some ease.

Yet again, he was in his office early and, at six a.m. on the dot, he was on parade and at his desk. He switched on his computer and, whilst it was responding, he walked over to the basin in the corner of the room and stared into the mirror above it. His face was still puffy with tiredness that did nothing to mask his overweight appearance, despite his new exercise routine. He felt and looked grey, from his hair and his moustache – Maybe the 'tache should go? he thought – to the pallor of his skin.

The strange fact that there was a basin in his office became less strange when you knew that the School had been a transit hospital in the Second World War and this had more than likely been a consulting room. Every morning now, the Bursar looked into the mirror and had the same thought: what must the army doctor have had to face each day as he washed his hands ready for the next patient – surely something far worse than merely a set of figures showing a terminal decline could ever be?

He walked back to his desk and looked at the spreadsheet on the screen. Only radical surgery would offer any hope of survival here, he thought.

He pressed Print as he needed to work on the figures for what he considered to be an important meeting, due to be held in the near future at the local hotel, which had been convened by the Great White Hope, as the Founder had sarcastically christened him, who had recently got involved in the School.

The GWH had emerged at a recent meeting – putting into effect one of the last suggestions from the Old Headmaster before he died – as one of two new non-executive directors, the other being the School Solicitor. A trusted family friend of the Old Headmaster, the GWH was, supposedly, a successful businessman who had run various companies and had the commercial track record to participate properly in the running of a school.

No, he had not had previous involvement in any kind of academic institution, but he had 'been to Oxford' and 'run a business' – therefore he was to be revered on Civvy Street just like a soldier who had been at the Battle of the Bulge would be in army circles.

The School Solicitor was seen largely as the Old Headmaster's man; they had got along famously and he had acted for him personally as well as for the School. The Founder also trusted him to look after the interests of the School – he and the Old Headmaster had seen eye-to-eye on that, just as they had done on so many issues. They both wanted the School to be able to continue after they were no longer around even though they knew that nobody would be quite as dedicated as they had been to its survival.

Nonetheless they both trusted the School Solicitor to be a worthy guardian of their ideals. He had been tremendously helpful to them both personally and, for a professional adviser, certainly showed loyalty to the School and shared their passion for its success.

Still, the Founder had occasionally wondered whether it was right that he should share a personal solicitor not only with the Old Headmaster but also with the School and so he had started consulting a hard-hitting partner in a rival firm, recommended to him by his personal bank manager.

Nothing wrong with keeping people on their toes! That should make sure he got the best kind of service for the School from the School Solicitor who clearly disapproved of his new choice of adviser, but whose professionalism prevented him from saying anything.

Fortunate then, that the School Solicitor was also the product of some minor public school: he probably was furious, but he couldn't let it show. He would know that if he put a foot wrong, he could be replaced. The Founder would keep him not just on his toes, but right up on tiptoes!

7

The Old Matron lived, ate and breathed the School and had been there right at the start, working in all its departments: the office, the sickbay, the classroom and even, on occasion, the canteen.

She knew everyone on the academic and the administrative staff. She knew every pupil and their parents. She knew every nook and cranny of the School buildings and grounds.

She had thrown herself into all aspects of the running of the School. She was, without doubt, private education's equivalent of the vicar's wife: there on Speech Day, glad-handing the parents; there at Sports Day handing over the prizes; helping out on trips; going on overseas recruitment tours; interviewing new members of staff; counselling any employee through personal difficulties; smoothing over issues between the Founder, the Bursar and the Old Headmaster; and doing all the stuff that would have given her an OBE if her contribution had been catalogued and written up in a citation.

Over the years, her role had changed as she fulfilled different functions. Now she was like the dowager at some landed estate: still living in a house in the grounds, but without any formal job role or clear responsibilities. She did not see it that way, of course. She carved out a 'guardian of our inheritance' function and was treated as such and involved in top-level meetings and decisions.

Those in charge of the School were not interested in what anybody else on the staff thought about the involvement of the Old Matron as she had been so involved for so long, it was assumed that, as she had had a lifetime's commitment to the School, she had a job for life working in and for it.

She still had great dignity and dressed to match. With her customary poise, she had introduced the two new members at an owners' meeting. In their role as non-exec directors, the School Solicitor and the GWH were there to safeguard and preserve the main asset, namely the School.

The GWH had arrived alongside the School Solicitor and they had slotted into place very neatly at the meeting – now styled a Board meeting – with one asking for the latest management accounts and forecasts and the other asking for an update on the new sports hall and the reports in the local press about delays, contract breaches and cost over-runs.

The Founder was confounded by this; he didn't expect questions from this gathering – he expected rubber-stamping, nods of heads and a quick exit to the village pub's restaurant for the usual gin and tonic to take the edge off the day, followed by a big-portioned lunch, all charged to the School's account.

It all seemed a bit Dickensian to the GWH, but if that was what owning the School was all about, he just had to go along with it and play the game.

The convivial lunch was more an exercise by the Founder in neutering opposition and in using sticky toffee pudding to bond any warring factions together. After all, it was a technique he had deployed all his working life, both in and out of the army. When he said, before lunch, that he would look into things, he could be sure that nobody would remember this commitment after it had been consumed.

In the pub car park after the lunch, the GWH had floated the suggestion of something he called a 'brain-storming strategic review' of the School so that a business plan could be written, giving the Bursar and the Acting Head milestones along a road to recovery.

The Founder supposed that the GWH must know what he was talking about, even though he had appeared at the meeting without a tie! Although it all sounded very airy-fairy, the Founder was delighted to go along with the notion – after all, if it happened at all, it would certainly kick any problems and any probings well and truly into the long grass.

8

As someone who was basically 'old school', the Founder was feeling rather confounded. This was all beginning to get to him. His family were urging him to do something with the School to try and retire, perhaps selling it on, and they pointed to the declining dividends as reason to cash in now, whilst it might be worth something.

With his wife dead, he felt rather alone and isolated, a feeling which regular visits from impecunious family members did little to assuage.

He tried to keep up appearances, but that was a battle he felt he was losing, although the outside world marvelled at his rather smart, clean clothes, his fastidious time-keeping and his ability to appear absolutely calm at all times.

He could feel his shoulders drooping by the day as his responsibilities wore him down. Still tall, but now elegantly stooped, he retained his air of effortless superiority.

His horn-rimmed glasses gave him a wise and owlish look, which, helped by his egghead baldness, lent him an academic and intellectual air and authority. Looks can be deceptive, he knew himself, but seeing how those he met treated him, and suspecting their illusions, he was happy enough never to correct them.

Over his daily mid-afternoon game of a rather complicated version of patience, he returned constantly to the feeling that life was more difficult than it used to be. Yes, he knew the world had moved on, but was it him, or did everything seem to have been made more difficult in the pursuit of apparent simplification and speed.

For instance, when he had set up the School, he had trundled along to his local bank manager, who had known his father as it happens, and merely explained that he wanted to buy a rather run-down stately pile and turn it into a school and that five thousand pounds would help.

The bank could not have been more helpful: the loan was agreed straight away, together with a new account opened immediately with a further five thousand pound overdraft facility in place by the afternoon. No guarantees required, no proof of identity – just a discussion about the business aims and objectives and the knowledge that the building was going to be a worthwhile asset.

Now, they faced constant demands from the bank about repayment of their outstanding loan, regular and giddy increases in interest rates and requests for management and audited accounts to be forwarded as soon as available. He had even, would you believe, recently been asked to provide copies of his passport and a utility bill as proof of identity!

When they had first opened the School doors for business, parents didn't ask for the latest inspection reports, food hygiene certificates and what child protection systems were in place, they just paid the bills and delivered the kids to the School, dumping them and disappearing.

Department for Education involvement was far less intrusive back then and health and safety, that twin-headed god of discombobulation, had not even made it onto the stage.

It all seemed so long ago when he had been in the army, when you could carry out orders, give orders expecting them to be obeyed and not have to refer everything to committees. He had realised he had been institutionalised, of course, by his military experiences and so it had felt entirely natural, when he resigned his commission, that he should think of setting up a school.

He had been to a very miserable one himself, from the age of six. It hadn't done him any harm! Far from it, it made joining the army seem like a step into freedom.

Dormitories – nothing to it. Communal wash facilities – jolly lucky to have them. Three meals a day – what more do you need? Uniform – made getting dressed a piece of cake.

And his school had given him the skill of being able to darn his own socks, probably the only other skill he had learnt there, apart from reading, which he still practised. He'd had to sew for himself, even when married, as his county wife, for all her social skills, had not really been able to do much of any domestic use apart from a bit of cordon bleu cookery, which she had learnt at a finishing school in Switzerland.

He had tried to set up the School to reflect his army life; basic, yes, but when you get everything 'all found', surely that was fine? Add in a bit of sound learning and you were bound to turn out decent, well-adjusted chaps, able to stand on their own two feet and make their way in the world.

Well, yes, things were starting to get more testing with new directives, new standards, new laws, and suchlike and, of course, the introduction of girls had brought with it a whole raft of problems. But nothing the School hadn't triumphed over.

He had had a real star in the Old Headmaster who had been in a good regiment and had made a damn fine officer. Once he had done his bit of retraining, he had taken over after the Founder had handed him the reins, a couple of years after the School had first opened its doors.

Now he felt that his buffer had been removed and he had been thrust once more into the front line. He didn't like that one little bit. It didn't make for clear thinking at all. All he really wanted to do was retire, properly, and not be bothered with it all, but he knew that as majority shareholder such an exit was a bit of a pipedream.

Well, maybe the idea proposed by the GWH that the Acting Head and the Bursar should draw up a business plan for the School wasn't such a bad idea. It could mean that they would be charged with carrying out the plan and held accountable for it. It's your plan. Take ownership of it. Bring it to fruition, he could hear himself telling them. And yes, they would be bloody well accountable if it failed.

9

THE NEXT DAY THE FOUNDER urged the Bursar to get the brainstorming day fixed and, after a few phone calls with the GWH and the Acting Head, the date was agreed.

In advance of that, the Bursar spent a small part of each day preparing for the session and tried to interest the Acting Head in chatting about it, suggesting they should get together to plan how they would deal with the meeting and what was likely to come up.

He finally popped along to the headmaster's study, a very impressive room at the corner of the house which looked down the garden to the wall in front of the ha-ha, the fields and distant hills, and also views across the rose garden towards the open-air swimming pool and the assault course in the copse beyond.

The first thing he noticed when entering the study was that the usual wax smell of the School also had top notes of a kind of ointment that he could remember from childhood. What was it? Friars' Balsam? Germolene? Some kind of camphor oil? Sloan's Liniment? An embrocation? Maybe even dubbin? He couldn't remember smelling any of it in the Old Headmaster's time, but still, perhaps it was just some fancy new-fangled fragrant candle.

'Good morning, sorry to disturb you,' he said to the Acting Head, who was seated facing the door with a portrait of the Old Headmaster looking down on him from its berth above the very ornate fireplace. 'Do you think we should make some time to discuss the brainstorming and how we should approach it?'

'Oh, no,' was the response. 'Let's see what His Cleverness has to say first. We should carry on as normal to show that we've nothing to fear and have everything under control.'

'But do we?' fretted the Bursar. 'I mean what do you think we should do about the falling numbers for the next academic year?'

'What we've always done... get the heads of our feeder schools in for a slap-up lunch and make sure we keep getting our successes on the sports field so that they carry on sending us their "all-rounders", eh!'

'But Headmaster (he heard himself drop the 'Acting' bit for the first time and instantly regretted it, even if he also knew that it was absurd to keep saying it), is that going to be enough? Can't we at least have a few other marketing ideas up our sleeve? Perhaps we should share the car journey there, at least, to get our story straight?'

'All right then. Good idea. On the day of the meeting, why don't you pick me up first thing from the School. That way I can have a glass at lunchtime, too, which will help me get through what is sure to be a very tedious day.'

Back in his own office, the Bursar sank back into a reverie, puzzled at how the School had got to this size and still seemed to stand or fall on the quality of its head. Surely a body such as this should have its own momentum? The staff members stayed pretty much the same and were educationally solid if a little uninspiring, and the backstage crew, as it were, in catering, 'matroning' and maintenance, were all loyal and long-serving.

Yet, he had a feeling that the School had drifted and would continue to drift without its previous captain at the helm, no matter what was being done to get it back on course.

10

The Bursar was surprised to have a call from the School Solicitor. It was usually the other way around: he sometimes had to call him to get his help with some contractual issue or to check the interpretation of an arcane piece of legislation. Inevitably something unpleasant to deal with, he guessed, would have necessitated a call the other way round.

Therefore, he was virtually standing to attention as soon as he realised who was calling.

Relieved to find that the School Solicitor only wanted to fix for himself and the GWH to pop in to see him later that week, when and if convenient, to have a chat and familiarise the GWH with the School and so forth, he was delighted to arrange a day and time as it would be light relief and a distraction from the usual day-to-day tedium of accounting and finance.

It offered some respite from the seemingly never-ending queries and requests for petty cash for this and that, or for urgent consideration to be given for money to be made available for equipment for the School, or its grounds, or to meet the demands of the sports hall.

Anyway, he liked the School Solicitor. He knew the Old Headmaster had relied on him for help and friendly advice about matters in general as well as on specific points of concern. He might be able to learn a bit more about how the directors viewed the School and their responsibilities. What worries and concerns did they have? Could he, should he, share any of his own with them?

He knew the School Solicitor had had a rich and varied life as a small-town solicitor and had run a successful practice that had recently moved into swanky new headquarters in the local town. Not only that, but he had only just handed over as senior partner, so knew something about managing change and relinquishing control to someone new and untested. It would be good to have the benefit of an outsider's viewpoint and experience, especially one with an insider's knowledge of the School and its history as well as a familiarity with most, if not all, of the people involved in the running of it.

The Bursar knew too that the School Solicitor's apparent pinstriped conformity hid a clear-headed, free-thinking man of principle who could usually be relied upon to see straight to the heart of any matter.

11

The Bursar was at the School well ahead even of his usual time on the day of the visit. He had woken up suddenly and very early with the thought that it was an inspection he was facing, but quickly settled back to dozing mode after it dawned on him that that was only his anxiety feeding his fears.

He had decided to give them the full works: a tour of the main building, the top dorms, the kitchen and dining room and then, after a coffee and chat back in his office, onto the main science, music and languages classrooms, then the new sports hall, the stable block sixth-form rooms and common room and, to round off, a visit to the School's farm. That should take them nicely up to lunchtime.

The visit started well; both guests turned up on time and independently remarked on how well the Bursar was looking. 'It's my new exercise regime,' he proudly replied. Must be working, he thought to himself.

And when asked, by way of follow-up pleasantry, what that regime involved, he could honestly reply, 'No biscuits and a walk round the School grounds at lunchtime. Nothing else. No cutting out of favourite foods. No loss of the evening scotch and soda either!'

After a coffee – with biscuits for the guests, but not the Bursar, of course – and an exchange of grumbles about the weather and the challenges of running any business in the nervous economic climate, the tour got underway.

It was all going fine until they went up the main staircase to the oldest of the dorms and the visitors (or were they now acting as 'inspectors'?) started asking about how recently the toilet and washing facilities had been renewed and when certain areas had last been redecorated.

They were obviously not impressed and he had hesitated before admitting that the answers were twenty years ago and eight years ago respectively. Some of the other dorms were, if anything, even shabbier, so he thought he had better state that the old house was in line for a major 'refurb' over the summer holidays.

Perhaps that part of the tour would have gone better too if Pupil A had not been in the dorm on his own, lying on his bed sobbing.

‘Whatever is the matter, boy?’ he asked the startled child.

‘Nothing, sir. Homesick, sir.’

‘You’d better cut along and get back to lessons. I’ll have to tell your housemaster about this – you know it’s against the rules to be up here at this time of day.’

‘Right, sir. Sorry, sir.’

Pupil A returned the framed photo of his parents to the stained bedside table and went sheepishly on his way. The Bursar was thrown by this, as he hated getting involved in pastoral stuff. In fact he disliked real contact with any individual child that he thought of as merely one of a number making up the total headcount.

He shared his distaste with his visitors: ‘Can’t stand it when pupils get all emotional – he’ll have to learn to control visible displays like that or he won’t last the course.’

The visit was losing momentum before it had really started, which was a pity. Still, onto the kitchen, which he prayed would be all shipshape and Bristol fashion.

He tried to ignore the glances exchanged between his guests and led the way back down the main staircase, across the waxed entrance hall and through the double doors into the dining hall.

They startled one of the kitchen porters who turned on his heel and rushed into the kitchen, doubtless to warn the catering manager. He hadn’t let the swing door close behind and they heard his warning cry of, 'I spy strangers.'

They followed him into what seemed to be a large, steam-driven kitchen where all the cooks and helpers stood strangely to attention.

The Bursar almost shouted 'at ease, men' but managed to stop himself and say 'carry on'. This seemed apt to introduce the clanging chaos of pans clanking on colanders as the cabbage was drained ready for the first sitting of lunch. That would explain the smell then.

Retreating from the kitchen war zone, the small group went back through the dining room to the Bursar's office. The assistant to the School secretary was on hand to provide coffee as soon as they sat down.

'Look, Bursar,' the School Solicitor opened, 'we wanted to have a chat with you and get to see the School on a typical working day.'

He got no further than that before the Acting Head burst in, clearly in a foul mood. 'What's going on here? I didn't know about this visit. Why wasn't I informed?'

More glances were exchanged between the guests whilst the Bursar explained in placatory tones that it was merely a 'fam' trip for the directors that he felt able to handle on his own, pretty much as he did with any major supplier or commercial contractor. 'It happens all the time, after all, so I thought nothing of it.'

'Well, make sure it doesn't disrupt the normal workings of the School.'

'Oh, I hardly think it will,' said the School Solicitor. 'People are quite used to seeing me, at least in the main areas, and my co-director looks quite friendly and promises only to look and learn.'

'That's just as well. Anyway, I'm sorry I can't stay, gentlemen. I'm due in the hall to help a prize pupil overcome his fear of public speaking. Can't have my rugger captain terrified of making a speech at the club dinner, can we?'

The Acting Head, having fizzed in, then fizzled out of the room, leaving an annoyed tableau of shrugging men looking at each other in a 'what was all that about' way. That had taken any enjoyment out of the visit and the rest of the tour was carried out with no great joy for any member of the party.

They had snuck in the back of a lesson being given in the language centre by the Head of English, who was teaching EFL to the pupils from overseas. He had written up on the blackboard (no fancy whiteboards here) in large letters '_ E N Y' and was asking the class if anyone knew what letter could go in front of the other three to make a word. There was no answer from the class, only an awkward silence. Then, you could hear the class questioningly whisper words beginning with different letters but all rhyming with 'penny'.

The teacher again asked the question, 'What letter do we need?' before finally losing patience and saying, 'It's a D. It's a D!'

'DEN-NY!' the class shouted out in unison.

The penny only dropped with both the class and the visitors when the teacher pronounced it correctly: 'Dee-nigh. DENY!'

The three interlopers then slipped out of the language lab – proudly described as such in spite of, rather than because of, its rather aged audio-visual equipment.

The lunch had been the only moment when normal relations were resumed, largely because the food served was really rather good, despite the earlier off-putting preview. This was partly because the stop-off at the School farm had lifted their spirits when they saw some of the farm class clearly getting a lot out of looking after the new lambs that had arrived earlier in the week. The Bursar had been able to proudly boast of the talent that could be discovered even in the most awkward child if given the opportunity – where perhaps the less academic could shine and develop skills that they didn't know they had.

———◆———

Meanwhile, a strange scene was unfolding in the smallish assembly hall, not to be confused with the sports hall, which was used for large-scale events. Pupil B was standing on the stage, with the Acting Head having taken up a position at the back of the hall.

'OK, when you're ready.'

Quietly, with head down, the boy mumbled, 'The First XV has enjoyed mixed fortunes this year. The results were: played 12, won 2, lost 9, with one match drawn – or should I say abandoned, sir?'

'Why?'

'Well, it was the blizzard game, sir. The one when the other team ran off the pitch and refused to return. The one where the away coach wouldn't stay for tea, sir, as he said you'd insulted them.'

'That's a victory in my book. Not a draw. You lot stood your ground.'

'Only because we didn't want detention, sir.'

'Never mind bleating about that. Actions have consequences. That's what you've all learnt. Now, again please and this time with more confidence.'

'Played 12, won 3, lost 9...'

'No! Not so half-hearted. Look, you're mumbling. You're looking down. Look up. PRO-JECT! You're looking embarrassed to be up there. You're the captain. You've got to inspire the team. You must rally the troops. We'll take it from the top and try a few techniques to make you less inhibited. Just jump down from the stage and I'll explain what I want you to do.'

12

After the visit (i)

THE ACTING HEAD CALLED ON the Bursar and demanded an explanation.

'Why was I excluded from that little knees-up?'

'You weren't excluded – I didn't think you'd want to be bothered with it.'

'That's for me to decide, don't you think, unless you preferred to have a private session with them?'

'Come off it. What do you take me for? You're just being paranoid!'

'Just because I'm paranoid doesn't mean they're not out to get me. Have you heard that one?'

'Well, not in my case. It's a straightforward misunderstanding. It won't happen again.'

'It had better not.'

After the visit (ii)

In the car park, the School Solicitor invited the GWH back to his house for tea.

'Well, that was all rather odd, wasn't it?'

'Very uncomfortable.'

'I'm still wondering why that boy in the dormitory was quite so upset.'

'Something and nothing, I expect. But did you see that child waiting by the front door as we left? His neck was covered in red blotches. I thought it was just a rash at first, but then realised that they looked like love bites. Most bizarre.'

'Yes, that certainly caught my eye too and I think you could be right.'

'Look, come back to the house and let's review where we are over a cup of tea before you head off back home.'

'Yes, I think we better had.'

13

THE SCHOOL SOLICITOR LIVED IN a delightful old farmhouse and he proudly showed off his newly restored granary, now being used as a pen for the few sheep that he and his wife kept, along with a *Good Life* number of chickens and other livestock.

'Actually, I think that these are better living quarters than those at the School,' the GWH observed.

'That's only a small part of my concerns for the School, but I must say, what an impression to give. It almost beggars belief.'

'It's a pity we don't run the place.'

'That's just it. We don't. We haven't got the authority to out-vote the Founder. Still, as non-execs we can make life a bit difficult for him, so we had better have a plan.'

They moved into the house and sat in the large kitchen at a round table by the window.

'What'll it be – tea or coffee? If it helps you decide, I've got a very good Sumatran roast which I can bung in the cafetière.'

'That sounds good to me.'

As they sipped their coffees, they discussed the School and their role as non-exec directors.

'We must remember why the Old Headmaster wanted us appointed – to make sure that the School was not broken up. There's the added weight of his Expression of Wishes, written when he wrote his will, where he made it plain that he wanted the School to continue as long as it was commercially viable.'

'That'll be awkward then, if we don't think it is! That's why it's so crucial to get a proper business plan in place; one that's sensible and achievable too. Even then we'll have to see whether it can be followed successfully.'

'You know, the Old Headmaster was always pretty realistic about the place; he knew it wasn't perfect, but he had a good grip on the finances and knew when to invest and when to save.'

'But how come the place has got into such a poor state of repair?'

'I think that's happened rather quickly, in the past couple of years whilst he was ill. Routine maintenance, which he was always such a stickler for, has been ignored because of the expense of building the new sports hall. He never wanted that, but it seems he was outmanoeuvred by the Founder and the Deputy Head, as he was then, who were banging on and on about how a modern private school had to have proper sporting facilities to compete for more applications. The Old Headmaster felt that sport was important, but not really what he wanted his School to be all about.'

'Isn't sport part of the public school ethos?'

'Well, the parents and the PE teachers think it is, but I've never been so sure about the children themselves!'

'The new sports hall doesn't seem to have been particularly well planned. For a start, it has broken with the School tradition of leaving a healthy cash reserve in place to cover a couple of problem years.'

'What about the time they bought The Old Rectory in the village to set up as a prep school. Didn't they do the same then and borrow from the bank?'

'That was a while ago, but looking at the old sets of accounts it seemed like they only spent some of the reserves, yes, but they borrowed the rest from the bank and paid it off over ten years, largely out of the extra fees they earned. Unlike the sports hall where they have largely spent all the reserves and then borrowed from the bank, The Old Rectory was an income-producing asset.'

'How serious is the financial state of the School in your view?'

'Actually, I think it's probably touch and go. For a start, unless they can arrest the decline in pupil numbers, it's going to be tricky to break even without more and more cost-cutting. On top of that, they need to fund repayments on the sports hall and, as we saw this morning, they really have to start a proper maintenance programme; the School is looking very tatty inside and out. And I've no idea about the School buildings. Looking at the windows, it's clear the outside needs a good paint and, judging by the damp on the dormitory ceilings, it looks likely that the roof needs attention.'

'We're certainly painting a gloomy picture, no pun intended!' The School Solicitor thought for a moment and then asked, 'What next? Where do we go from here?'

'I think the business plan is important for two reasons: we can address the main issues facing the School and its survival and, at the same time, consider whether the time has come to sell up as opposed to carrying on.'

'God, I don't know how the Founder would feel about that. He'd probably have a fit if he knew we were even talking that way.'

'I can't see how else to approach it. When I have the brainstorming session, I'll focus on the plan and the development of the School. That gives us a chance to see whether it's realistic with the current set-up to carry on or to blow the whistle and look at other options.'

'What's your view of the management of the School? As I've said, it was all right a few years ago when the Old Headmaster ran the place – it seemed to work well as he had a vested interest in the financial success as well as the academic success; the two went hand in hand. That's all changed now and I'm not even sure the Acting Head has access to all the figures. He surely won't know just how much profit the School has made in the past. He'd be another one having a fit if he knew that!'

'Well, the management structure is poor in my view and you've hit the nail on the head in saying that what the business does and how its finances work have to be managed in tandem. The Acting Head probably knows more than we think, but that needs to be formalised, even with a profit-share maybe.'

'Good luck with that! Sharing profits with non-shareholders is a no-no with the Founder.'

'He'll have to face the facts though. I think there should be a proper Board set up – I'm shocked really that there's no academic-experienced director involved. The meetings of the owners fall way short of what even a traditional Board of Governors does at other schools. It's OK to have a shareholders' meeting, but day-to-day management should be in the hands of a properly constituted Board. Either the Acting Head or the Bursar needs to be managing director or, together, they could even be joint MDs.'

‘Are they up to that?’

‘Well, we can see what happens over the next month or so with the business plan process and how they rise, or not, to the challenge.’

Conversation meandered slightly after that, largely around the type of people that the Bursar and the Acting Head were. The Bursar was categorised as solid and dependable, but perhaps lacking in wider commercial and business skills. Still, it was felt that he could be a useful foil to the Acting Head, who was an unknown element in all this.

Yes, there was the largely negative view from the Old Matron, but he was championed by the Founder. As to the views of the staff, not much was known and maybe soundings should be taken. He was certainly keen on the sporting side of things and was totally committed to working long hours for the good of the teams, not only giving up evenings and weekends but also organising British and overseas rugby and cricket tours during the holidays.

If dedication were enough, they concluded, the School was in safe hands.

———◆———

At the same time as this meeting was taking place, the parents of Pupil C drove slowly up the School’s long drive in their new Maserati. It was their day to see their son and take him out to the local hotel for afternoon tea. Might as well give their latest car an outing, and test whether the fuel consumption was as bad as the garage had boasted.

They were a successful couple. A big mortgage admittedly, and one made larger with two or three remortgages, but they lived in a huge house and had managed to get all their offspring into boarding schools, each one carefully chosen by their education planner with the aim of bringing the best out in their children.

They had wanted a large family and they had wanted to be able to afford to send them all away to school so that they did not interfere with their own enjoyment of life. For him, this was working in banking, which he loved, even if it meant he could not be relied on to always make these visits. Work comes first. That was the agreement with his wife.

She herself had given up her 'high-flying' (as she put it to anyone she met) job in the City to concentrate on running the home and the family. Equally, her priority had been to ship the kids off to school and convince them that full boarding was the only way forward. No one could ever quite understand just how high-powered she had been and she had long given up trying to explain her glittering career to the poorer parents she seemed constantly to come across.

'These grounds are second to none, aren't they? You can tell this whole place is run by military types,' observed the father.

His wife could only agree. 'The facilities are good; no doubt about it. I'm glad we chose this school. Think of the friends he'll make. The contacts. The networking. Half the children here are incredibly wealthy. You know one of them has pocket money of two thousand pounds a week? There's one in his dorm who is practically landed aristocracy!'

Her husband had glazed over and was gazing at the grounds when he was momentarily distracted.

'What's going on over there?'

'Where?'

'There!'

'Which way?'

'Over there, in the trees.'

'I can't see anything.'

'It looked like someone had tied a boy to a tree and the others were dancing around him.'

'Oh don't be so ridiculous! It's probably the assault course. You know perfectly well that they use the woods for their Combined Cadet Force training exercises. They've got two brigadiers' sons here, haven't they?'

'It looked like something out of *Lord of the Flies* to me.'

14

The day of the brainstorming meeting had finally dawned and the Bursar, after his usual fitful night's sleep, was up and about early, waiting outside the Acting Head's house in the School grounds until the pre-arranged eight a.m. pick-up time. Slightly after eight, which increased the Bursar's anxiety a further notch, out came his passenger clutching a bulging briefcase.

'What's in the briefcase?' only gained a wink and a tap on the side of the nose.

'Just a few papers on my plans for the School.'

'Don't you think they should have been discussed beforehand in the last owners' meeting?'

'Oh don't worry about that. I thought we should get some input today before finalising what we want to do.

We should be the ones presenting any outcomes from today's session and this should ensure that's the case.'

'I thought this was going to be a free-flowing brainstorm – sounds to me like you're trying to hijack it.'

'Look, you've got to play the game in all this management consultancy lark. We can't have them telling us what we should be doing. At least this way we'll be telling him what he should be telling us!'

The short journey passed in silence and the driver was grateful that the morning rush hour gave him the excuse of having to concentrate on his driving so he made no pretence at chit-chat.

His passenger stared ahead rather smugly.

15

The GWH had arrived early at the hotel, which had meant a very early start to the day. He was already tired before the meeting began. He checked the small meeting room after introducing himself to the banqueting assistant who would be looking after them for the day.

He had confirmed the coffee and pastries on arrival, with replenishment at eleven, and that they would take lunch in the restaurant at one. They would be finishing at three-thirty with tea and biscuits.

When he went into the room, he was grateful it had a window to the outside world – so often conference rooms used otherwise unusable space to give a Black Hole of Calcutta feel, which certainly didn't encourage an open mind when you couldn't even open a window.

No sooner had the welcome coffee arrived than his 'guests' strode in, full of confidence and bluster. The GWH, sporting his familiar open-necked shirt, was in stark contrast with the Bursar and the Acting Head who were more formally dressed. It was obvious in their meeting of eyes that each thought the other inappropriately attired.

Straight away you could tell that the Acting Head was quite happy to schmooze and clearly considered himself 'charm on legs', arm outstretched, hand ready to shake, like a canvassing politician on the scrounge for a few extra votes, which, of course, in a way, he was.

His sole goal for the day was that he came out of it well. He would listen, he would be reasonable, he would cede ground, he would consider suggestions and argue calmly any contentious point, whether or not he had been the one raising it.

Above all, he would try and ensure that nothing emerged that had the stamp of 'we hadn't thought of doing that before'.

As soon as they had exchanged a few pleasantries and traffic reports and the coffee was poured, they sat down. 'Well, what is the agenda for the day?' asked the Acting Head.

There is always an agenda for a meeting or, more precisely, there are always many agendas for a meeting. Everyone attending has their own 'hidden' agenda, whether it is to get through the meeting unnoticed or to try and get a pet project green-lit.

Top of the hidden agendas for this meeting were, for the GWH, to try and find out what the Acting Head and the Bursar were made of and whether they were up to their jobs. Did the School have a hope of surviving in their hands? For the Acting Head, it was not to be railroaded into anything he didn't agree with. Who was the headmaster around here? The Bursar wanted to make sure that everyone was clear about where they were trying to get to next and avoid any shortfall in fees being blamed on him. Oh, and is there any way the School can make a profit next year?

The official agenda, as presented by the GWH, read simply:

Brainstorming Day
Agenda

Morning: Intro
- *Roles and responsibilities*
- *Goal: to prepare a 3-year business plan for the School*
- *Stages – agree timescale for putting the plan together and establish what the required end-product should be*
- *Theme: 'Securing the Future'*
    - *Securing the business*
    - *Securing the succession*

- *Securing profitability – most important (will enable us to satisfy the aims of the School and secure its future!)*
- *SWOT analysis of Strengths, Weaknesses, Opportunities, Threats*

Lunch

Afternoon
- *How to put the plan together – who does what?*
- *Figures and requirements*
- *Implementation issues*

The GWH introduced the agenda and tried to stress that his role was that of a 'facilitator', although the other two were very clearly and deeply sceptical about this, cynical about his sincerity and paranoid about what and to whom he would be reporting back about the day.

They worked through the agenda as if there weren't any hidden agendas, which stayed, therefore, hidden, as is customary on such occasions.

The Acting Head demonstrated a good grasp of the headline figures, even more so than the Bursar, whose head was so full of figures from past years, the current years and forward forecasts, that even he could see that he was in danger of not seeing the wood for the trees.

There were times he confused gross profit with net profit and forgot to deduct the owners' dividends before revealing some of the past years' profits. The raised eyebrows of the Acting Head alerted him to that mistake which he hurriedly corrected.

The Acting Head felt that the pupil roll would be stronger for the Autumn Term and that, no, he didn't imagine for a moment that they would be losing children to other schools. He also believed that morale amongst the staff and children was very high, which bode well for teacher and pupil retention next year.

It was with some confidence that he felt the School would soon be back in the black and he had no qualms about being able to meet the next tranche of debt repayment for the new sports hall.

The discussions went from the detailed – on fees, number of pupils at each stage in the School and staff costs, to the broad – about the nature of private education and how the state of the economy and government rules might impact the future for public schools.

It is surprising just how much can be covered and discussed in a day's meeting although even with just three participants, trying to move forward in agreement was problematical to say the least.

The flip-chart came to the rescue. At periodic intervals, the GWH would jump up, grab a felt tip pen and, partly to wake himself up a bit and partly to try and win some consensus for an issue, he would summarise a few points so that they could agree and move on.

At the end of the meeting, the GWH ceremoniously took the large flip-chart pad and rolled it up. He presented this to the Bursar and the Acting Head and said, 'Look, in my experience, these notes and summaries are a great help in drawing up the plan. After all, they capture the essence of what was said under each topic – a good reference point for what we discussed.'

The first page had these words on them:

Roles and responsibilities

For the plan

- *Past figures – the Bursar with analysis*
- *SWOT analysis – the AH and Bursar with all staff input*
- *Future projections – AH and Bursar, with assumptions including capital requirements, staffing levels, pupil numbers and fee levels*
- *Marketing initiatives and expected results, with timescale – AH with Head of Geography (PR and recruitment)*
- *Regulatory and educational – the AH – likely changes and development issues and how to exploit for pupil numbers growth*
- *Strategy – AH and Bursar – the 5-year plan, the target markets, the methods of achieving the target turnover and net profit*
- *Summary – the AH*
- *Timescale – end of the month – first draft*

– *Review meeting*
– *End of third month – final draft*

Day-to-day
– *Legal and financial – the Bursar*
– *Educational and pastoral – the AH*
– *Monthly financials for the Board – the Bursar*
– *Pupil recruitment – the AH*
– *Staff information – Bursar and AH*
– *Support staff – Bursar*
– *Catering – Bursar*
– *Buildings and grounds maintenance – Bursar*

The overriding reaction of the GWH to the way the meeting went was that the Bursar and the Acting Head really cared about the School. After careful tutoring, or maybe mentoring would be a better way of describing it, he felt that perhaps they could, between them, bring a three-year business plan together and present it to the owners.

Even the Bursar's worries about pupil numbers and his concerns about the likely need for capital expenditure on the School buildings seemed to have been swept aside by the confidence exuded by the Acting Head and his assured performance in his role, as he saw it, as 'academic, pastoral and commercial guardian of the School'. 'The

School will go from strength to strength on my watch,' he boldly announced at the end of the meeting.

The Bursar, at least, seemed convinced, although he had just announced his decision to retire the following year. So was he really that convinced by the Acting Head's proud claims, or was he just happy to go along with them because he would not be around to pick up the pieces if it all went pear-shaped?

16

As he drove home, the GWH, bored with the radio, tried the only hands-free activity available to him given that he did not feel like singing or reciting poetry – and that was thinking. He tried to amuse himself by building on a minor element that had occurred to him during the meeting.

Sometimes, the only way to get through some meetings or conferences was to latch on to a comic strand to puncture the tediousness of the proceedings. Once, he had sat through a serious employment law event, smiling internally because the chairman had been referred to in the conference papers, thanks to a misprint, as 'Joint Arthur' of a leading legal textbook. That had certainly undermined the seriousness of the occasion and made the chairman's smugness almost bearable.

He chuckled at the thought that at today's meeting, when he was writing 'Head of Geography' on the flip-chart, he had realised its abbreviated form was 'HOG'. So then, he thought in the car, the Head of History was 'HOH', the Head of English was 'HOE', and so on through 'HOC' and 'HOM' until he came to the Head of PE and decided that 'HOPE' was a good place to stop.

It was made a bit funnier by having met a few of the teachers and their new 'names' seemed to fit. Take the HOG, who was also helping with PR. He had boasted that, 'All you have to do to get the School into the local paper is take their rather dishy features editor out for a slap-up lunch and, bingo, you get your story straight in.'

The GWH wondered what the connection was between the HOG and the Acting Head; a strange friendship, given that they were two very different characters. Or were they?

He knew they were both passionate about rugby and it was now emerging that they were both keen on marketing and PR. On top of the HOG's teaching and pastoral care duties, the Acting Head had clearly wanted him to be the staff member allocated to assist him in promotional activities when he had stressed in the meeting the need for fresh impetus to be given to marketing to develop the School. He had said that it was fortunate that they were both involved with the rugby side of things as they had ample time together on the match buses to discuss ways of building activity to promote the School and attract new pupils. It seemed a strange way to while away the journeys, but, well, maybe it demonstrated a certain enthusiasm.

The GWH hoped they did not see their handling of PR and marketing as a passport to expense account wining and dining. Still, marketing had seemed to be an important dimension for the Acting Head and you could not really argue with that. He clearly blamed the lack of any previous proper professional planning in that area.

At the meeting he had, what is more, been quick to point the finger at the Board, as he called it in an obviously 'us' and 'them' way, for its lack of skills in that area and its failure to support him and the Bursar, 'It's all very well to push more and more responsibilities onto us, but what do they actually contribute in management terms? Sod all if you ask me!'

You could not really argue with that. But he had been wrong in his aside over lunch, which put it that, 'As long as they get a dividend, they don't really care what happens.' He had had to be corrected on that one.

The Bursar had put his heart and soul into the School and had shown himself at the meeting to be ready to do the same in drawing up a decent plan. His thoughtfulness throughout the day had been first class and his knowledge of the School's figures and structure, as well as his detailed familiarity with all the staff, was quite incredible, despite a few flustered lapses.

The Acting Head was seemingly at odds with the Bursar whose natural support he could easily have counted on, but he seemed determined to almost mock the older man's commitment and thoroughness.

It was going to be tricky to get a decent plan out of those two, thought the GWH, and it's going to be vital to get a decent replacement for the Bursar who will leave a hell of a hole when he goes.

He went back to listening to the radio.

Enough of hands-free thinking!

17

ONE THING WAS BEGINNING TO get the Founder down: the Acting Head kept buttonholing him when he popped into the School for a spot of lunch or a natter with the Bursar about the old army days. He also kept ringing him up at odd points during the day – and sometimes even after school and at weekends – with a never-ending stream of questions and observations, even to report on the School's Saturday sport results.

How could he tell the Acting Head that no, he didn't want to be bothered or to get involved, no matter whether he had said he would always be available for advice and happy to help. Surely you didn't have to spell it out that you were just being polite; just like bumping into someone in town and rounding off an awkward exchange with, 'We must get together for lunch sometime' when, good God, you'd rather go to the dentist and knew the other chap felt the same.

He realised that the Acting Head was perhaps only being deferential – trying to keep him informed and 'in the loop', but really, it seemed like he himself needed constant reassurance, even about some piffling little matter or other that was too trifling to mention and certainly too trivial to discuss.

It seemed to the Founder that the Acting Head had a lot to say about other people and most of it not very nice. Was he seeking to share his views so that he could elicit support for them? Was he trying to put down markers to influence the Founder's opinion of the people concerned? Or was he trying to test the Founder's reaction to assess what the Founder felt about certain individuals, so that he could plan some dastardly scheme to get them out?

And just what had the latest call really been about?

'The GWH was very helpful at the brainstorming, but we all know he has his own agenda, of course,' the Acting Head had reported back the evening of the meeting, even though he himself hadn't really thought that during the day.

'And what might that be, do you suppose?'

'Oh well, I guess he just wants to make sure that his interests are protected at all costs.'

'Wouldn't you say that his interests are the same as my interests then?'

'I can't really say for sure. He was a bit coy about the detail.'

Despite the Founder knowing from his army days that a report-back should be factual and detailed – ideally about follow-up action needed – and that those who liberally sprinkled such reports with personal asides and snide remarks could not really be trusted, it was difficult to avoid being affected by what was said, even if you knew the motives were questionable.

The Acting Head knew he had the ear of the Founder and he was careful to make sure that the poison he dripped was sweet-talked and not too acid-tongued.

18

On the Monday, after a bit of phoning round the other Board members, the Founder had a majority to support his notion of appointing the Acting Head as the new headmaster.

The idea had been that they should wait for the plan to be presented and, in the meantime, consider all options – but what was the point of that? The plan process was underway after all. Better to give authority now, to strengthen the development of the plan and its eventual implementation – once the plan had been accepted by the Board, of course.

Recruitment of pupils had to start right away and so did the hunt for a new bursar. It made sense to get the appointment of a headmaster over and done with.

The Founder felt energised by this, even though, if he was being honest with himself, it was driven by the aim of having a fully responsible headmaster who could take decisions and get on with things without bothering him.

It'll be the making of the Acting Head. Give him the confidence to stand on his own two feet and stop him treading on mine, he thought to himself.

No sooner had he got the support he needed than he phoned the Acting Head to tell him the news. The new Headmaster, as he now was, expressed 'profound gratitude' and gave almost an oath of obedience in his 'vow to be the best head the School has ever had'.

The only negative feedback he had received had been the Bursar saying, 'Well, if you're sure he's the right man for the job.'

Why did he care? He was retiring soon anyway.

That didn't stop the Founder sending out, the very next day, a letter to all staff and parents:

The Board has concluded, after much debate, that it is of paramount importance that we go into the campaign to settle the School and build on its success with a new headmaster at the earliest opportunity.

The Acting Head has shown his mettle in recent months and has the leadership qualities needed to take the School forward.

I know he has the support of all staff members and the popular support of parents. The timing is right, at this moment, to make this appointment a permanent one. It is not goodbye to the Acting Head but hello to the new Headmaster!

I am sure we all wish the new Headmaster every success.

19

THE BURSAR AND THE HEADMASTER had divided the chore of preparing the plan and they both got on with it, the Bursar with more willingness and commitment than the Headmaster, who was already completely taken with his new-found status.

Business cards were ordered straightaway and the School stationery amended and sent off for printing. No need to change 'Headmaster' on his study door as 'Acting' had never been added – the door had always recognised his authority.

All staff and pupils were instructed to call him 'Headmaster' at all times and never to use his name, even if writing notes to him. He liked it when passing staff members said 'Good morning, Headmaster', or when a nervous pupil tried to get round him in the corridor with 'Excuse me please, Headmaster'. He especially liked it when the rugby team trooped out of the changing room in single file with a leaving nod and a mumbled 'Headmaster'.

Perhaps it's gone a bit to my 'head', he chuckled to himself as he settled down one evening to work on the narrative of the plan. He started by looking at the stuff written by the Old Headmaster in one of the faded brochures prepared for overseas recruitment trips, where even the photos had a colonial quality to them.

We use our skills as educationalists to close the gap between attainment and potential.

I can re-use that, but this next bit will put parents off with its worthiness and honesty, he thought to himself.

We have continued to persevere with an educational approach that offers new opportunities to pupils who might otherwise have been regarded as failures. We have persevered [there was certainly a lot of 'perseverance', he thought] *in our belief that a pupil's true potential is often hidden behind a mask of poor academic achievement and that, in order to reach a balance between performance and potential, the pupil's self-image has to be made more positive.*

He knew he'd have to get away from that for a start or the School would be linked with failure.

He felt fortunate that the GWH had given them a template for the plan during the brainstorming day and once he settled into the writing of his sections, he quickly got into his mental stride. After a few hours, he was comfortable that he had broken the back of it and reviewed his efforts with some pride.

He didn't really believe in all this strategy stuff, but he had managed to put a convincing scenario down on paper. Guff really, he knew, but it all sounded pretty good, even if it was full of buzz words he had culled from a management article in the *Times Ed*.

After all, it had to be understood that the development of the School over its first decades had not been the result of a long-term strategy, carefully budgeted and methodically carried out. Availability of cash had played a bigger part than anything else. It had been 'flying by the seat of the pants' and not careful planning.

The trick now was to pass it all off as sound and achievable. As Headmaster, he knew he had the authority that would be difficult to challenge. How unbelievably daft of the Founder to confirm him as the head before he had presented his plan for the School! Another hurdle successfully jumped. And no mention of the matter that the Old Headmaster had obviously kept completely to himself! Phew!

20

THE BOARD MET TO RUN through and agree the School plan.

The Headmaster had placed himself at the head of the table, naturally. He had got in especially early to set up the table placements and had even beaten the Bursar in that morning, who himself had been an early riser and arrived in a state of nervous apprehension.

'For goodness sake, get yourself a coffee, Bursar, and try and relax. You look like a new recruit on his first day. There's nothing to worry about. The plan looks good, it reads well. You've worked your socks off on all the figures and graphs. Time to get some credit now for a job well done.'

'We've made a lot of assumptions in those figures. What if we're grilled and they expose the flaws?'

‘Are you kidding? This lot will be nodding along or nodding off. Either way, we’ve got nothing to fret about. Just leave the talking to me. I’ll cue you in if I need some financial blurb. Now you go off and gather all the plans together, whilst I go and do assembly. My theme is ‘A man’s reach must extend his grasp’. I think I heard it in a Kirk Douglas film on TV last weekend, *Ace in the Hole*.’

‘Isn’t it a Robert Browning quote, Headmaster?’

‘I don’t know about that. I’m not Head of English!’

Soon after ten a.m., the Bursar and the Headmaster were back in the meeting room waiting for the Board members to arrive. They trickled in over the next half an hour and stood around with their coffees and biscuits waiting for the ten-thirty start.

The Founder called them all to attention and the meeting was underway, with everyone but the Headmaster listening intently to the introductory reminiscences: ‘When the School started, there were only a handful of pupils and we didn’t have a written plan at all – and no ridiculous rules and regulations. We could even excavate the swimming pool with boy labour that saved us a fortune and taught them a great deal. Money was short and we only survived thanks to the army’s generous ‘Golden Bowler’ retirement package, which I ploughed into the School…’

The Headmaster had heard all this before so he focused on his own presentation, which he was feeling increasingly confident about. He did not like to admit it, even to himself, but the GWH had been a great help in refining the content and, so far, had modestly not referred to his mentoring role in making sure the plan stood up and read well.

He would make sure he thanked the GWH and the many other members of staff for their input – that would dilute the importance of the GWH's contribution, which, if he was honest, had been rather crucial. But he would not be honest.

He glanced at the contents page:

Executive Summary
Background
Main Products and Services
Marketing
Organisation and Personnel
Premises and Equipment
Catering and Maintenance
Financial
Management

How professional was that, he thought. He liked the idea of the School having a product to market. The GWH hadn't liked that one, but he had stuck to his guns. He liked, even more, the sub-section headed 'Command and Control' to introduce the concept of a Board of Directors and an executive management team.

Most of all, he was looking forward to reading out the quote he had put on the outside cover:

'*The old order changeth, yielding place to new...*' (*Morte d'Arthur*, Alfred Lord Tennyson)

That should lay down a marker.

He heard his name being called and stood to attention to claim his audience. Built like a rugby forward, he had an intimidating, in-your-face manner – the type who would argue with the referee.

He cut an imposing figure and despite his hair being a stranger to the comb, he looked the part, with his gown (not his), his blue shirt, the School tie and a TA badge on his blazer lapel.

The presentation went well. A few silly questions, which had the Bursar umming and ahhing, helped pass the time. Some suggestions he acknowledged as 'helpful', but had no intention of acting on, whilst others were a trifle hostile with some even challenging the CEO and headmaster roles being combined.

The bold plans to increase the pupil roll were well received as was the proposed increase in fees, which together with holding the staff headcount at around the hundred mark would yield a very good net profit, or 'surplus' as the Founder chipped in.

The plan ran to forty pages with annexes and lists and the discussion on it lasted a good two hours.

In the end, the Headmaster asked for a vote, which had taken the Founder by surprise, and the School Solicitor had asked for time to consider it in more detail. By then a majority had put their paws in the air to signify approval and that was good enough for the Headmaster. In his view, there had been no need for the Founder to tactfully suggest that any dissenting comments should be submitted in writing by the end of the following week.

Sherry was then served as a prelude to lunch and the Headmaster could mingle freely with the Board and with the senior teachers he had invited in for the social part of the proceedings.

The HOG was holding forth on the success of the First XV to the School's auditor, himself a big, burly second-row stalwart of the local rugby club. The Headmaster, gravitating to his own comfort zone, went over to join them.

'By the way, I've appointed myself head coach and physio, so we should see our results improve even more,' he offered as his contribution to the rugby chat and his status had granted him the ears of the other two.

'Physio, Mr Headmaster?' growled the auditor.

'Well, yes. I did a weekend course a while back and I realised we can't leave the matron to pick up the pieces after every match. There are a lot of knocks in every game and recovery is helped enormously if any minor injuries, bruising and muscle strains are dealt with straight away – sometimes in the dressing room right after a game or on the coach coming back from an away fixture. That's where I come in with my Sports Injuries Diploma.'

'A diploma? In a weekend?' a clearly nonplussed auditor queried.

'Well, not a formal diploma, you understand. But as good as, especially with all my many years of practical experience. It just formalises what I've always done for the boys.'

'We never did any of that in my day. A few bottles of beer after the game, care of the games master, was the best medicine for us back then.'

'The old order changeth, I'm pleased to say, so we'll do it my way if you don't mind!'

With that, the Headmaster turned away just as the gong went to summon them to the lunch table.

21

'WHAT ON EARTH WAS THE HEADMASTER on about with all that physio malarkey?' the auditor asked the HOG when they were seated at the table.

'Oh, he's frightfully good at all that sort of thing. He's got this special ointment – liniment, I think he calls it. I saw him work a miracle once on the rugger captain on the way back to the School from some tournament or other. The boy was complaining like hell about being hardly able to walk after some bruising tackle. The Headmaster had the boy strip down to his boxers so that he could rub this cream on his thigh and, blow me, the lad was saying it was much better in no time at all and was up in a whip-stitch, hoofing it to his mates at the back of the bus.'

‘I thought liniment was something you rubbed on horses?’

‘Racehorses, rugger buggers, they’re all thoroughbred, highly strung animals needing careful handling to get them to perform well. Same goes for the cricket and hockey wallahs come to that. And they get the same treatment.’

‘The Headmaster takes it all very seriously, I must say. Good for him. He’ll do the School proud.’

‘He certainly has a magic touch with the boys.’

‘Let’s see if it can rub off on the figures as well!’

22

THE HEADMASTER AND THE HOG lost no time at all in contacting the local newspaper to arrange a feature on the 'exciting new plans' for the School. That should show the old order what they are in for as well as make a decent splash locally for present and future parents. They did not think that parents and pupils past would take more than a passing interest.

The duly arranged lunch went off very well, they thought, and the bottle of Pinot Noir had certainly oiled the wheels. The local journalist had not been that impressed with the School's representatives, but she knew she had to humour them because her editor had told her that she would have to, in order to safeguard the advertising the newspaper received throughout the year from the School.

When they had met up – typical that it had to be a boozy lunch, she thought – she had clocked their clothes, or should that be their uniform, straight away.

In turn, the Headmaster in his blazer and the HOG in his sports jacket had noticed her blue jeans (as her editor had warned her that they would). Neither side commented, although they dearly would have loved to have done so.

She had smiled in all the right places, she thought, and nodded encouragingly throughout. They had not minded the use of the tape machine, so that meant she needed only to make the occasional note and concentrate on giving the impression that she was hanging on their every word.

It was during the lunch that the angle she would take fell into her mind and so did a possible headline: 'Best in class? New plan to relaunch leading private school'.

She was impressed that they had brought with them quite a few black and white photos, courtesy, they said, of the sixth-form photography club. These showed the front of the School with the Headmaster standing by the imposing front entrance holding the door open, as if to welcome a new arrival.

That would do for the main photo to accompany the article, she thought. Then a sprinkle of other shots of the grounds, a science lab and the School farm – that should give the variety needed.

The Headmaster was quickly into his stride about how the intention was to reinvent the School. It would focus on subject and sport achievements, on the development of well-rounded young adults ready to make their way in the world. The School would invest in infrastructure and in its staff and would market itself, but not aggressively, as they would let its merits speak for themselves, but in a carefully planned way.

Yes, they answered, advertising would form part of the 'marketing mix', as they put it, but they were very interested in developing advertorial. The HOG, who was well known to her even if his nickname wasn't, took the lead on all the PR jargon-inspired talk and she tried to get behind the bold claims to try and find out exactly what was going to be new and different.

This seemed to be more in terms of management changes than educational innovations and 'strictly off the record', the Headmaster made some pretty vicious jibes at the fuddy-duddy world of the old regime, or *ancien régime* as he kept calling it, unaware of the irony that by doing so, he was demonstrating that he himself was part of it.

They both seemed very keen on the whole team sports ethos that they intended to promote within the School and within the community, with access to their sports hall hailed as their 'passport to success' with these endeavours.

The Headmaster seemed inordinately proud of his success with his rugby teams and explained that you had to get close to the players to get the best out of them or, in his words, create a 'Games Bond' through which you would get a 'Licence to Win'. He seemed so pleased with himself, smug in fact, at coining that phrase that it made her all the more determined not to use it in the piece.

After an hour or so of this she had had quite enough and, feigning a pressing and prior engagement, made her excuses and left, saying she had so many nuggets of pure gold on tape that the article was almost going to write itself.

'Well, let's see how that one comes out,' the Headmaster said to the HOG after she had left.

'A fantastic start to our PR campaign, Headmaster,' came the loyal reply.

23

THEY DID NOT HAVE TO wait long to see their efforts rewarded in print. The column inches would be more than they could have ever hoped. A double-page spread! Well, almost, if you discounted the bottom half of one page advertising the local school clothing shop – 'For all your school garment requirements', and the bottom half of the other page advertising the town's leading financial adviser who was offering school fee packages – 'For parents and grandparents to give your precious ones a head start'.

Of course, they were not the first to see the article.

That misfortune had fallen on the Bursar. Up early, again, he had stopped on his way in to the School to buy the local paper that came out every Friday. Something to read over a cup of coffee, he had thought to himself, as he parked by the newsagent's shop in the square.

He didn't glance at it until he was at his desk. He opened the paper and nearly spilled his coffee in shock as he saw a picture of the Headmaster – as large as life – with the headline:

NEW HEADMASTER – OPENING THE DOOR TO CHANGE

With big plans to revitalise town's top private school

'What on earth?' shouted the Bursar into the empty room as he started reading:

... sees his role as the new Headmaster very much as a new broom: 'The changing of the guard means we can freshen everything up. We can tackle our performance in academic subjects as well as get behind the vocational side of things at which we can really excel.

'The Board has accepted my wide-ranging plans to ginger everything up, with a budget for growth and development, including a new marketing and PR allocation of funds to drive pupil recruitment here, there and everywhere.'

It certainly seems that this famous school with its reputation for getting the best out of all of its pupils is in for a big shake-up. The plans (which are obviously extremely confidential, given that competition for fee-paying pupils is a cut-throat business) are comprehensive. I was lucky enough to be shown a copy and, in a wide-ranging discussion, was guided through it by the Headmaster himself and a senior colleague.

They clearly have big plans and are wasting no time in implementing them.

'Building on the sporting reputation of the School and its investment in its state-of-the-art sports hall, we are going to recruit the best players in all sports and offer generous sporting scholarships. We have first-rate facilities to offer and it would be a sin if they were not being used by first-class athletes and sportsmen.'

I asked how previously announced plans to increase the level of female intake into the School might be affected by this push.

'Not at all. We will have domestic science classes run by the School's catering team so that all options are covered.'

When I clarified that I meant whether sports facilities included female sports and the hope to recruit top-performing female athletes, the Headmaster had this to say:

"Of course! Hockey and netball clubs will be developed and the Head of English hopes to start a lacrosse team next year. We already have a strong community of horse-riding girls so that will be built up to include our own stabling and use of part of our thirty-six acres of agricultural and recreational grounds. But we won't be doing things like girls' cricket, rugby or football, thank you very much!'

In conclusion, I asked the Headmaster whether all the extra expenditure was affordable in the current economic climate. We had touched on the fact that all over the country, public schools were closing because of falling pupil rolls. But it seems that nothing can dent the new Headmaster's confidence in what he can achieve.

'I hope to be the best head that this School has ever had and the best thing to happen to the School since it was founded all those years ago.'

Part of the fund- and profile-raising effort will be to promote the School's Summer Ball, which is usually held only every five years. With the next one only weeks away, the Headmaster said to me: 'We want the local paper to be there, with its leading journalist and photographers, on one of our sponsored tables – which I can let you have at a discount, of course – as I want you to see the vibrancy of the School, the support we get from the parents and, of course, give us a good write-up with photos afterwards.'

The Bursar was standing up at this point, muttering, 'How can he be so foolish and loose-tongued. What on earth will the Founder say to this? What will our parents make of it?'

24

THE POST-MORTEM GOT UNDERWAY that morning and lasted for the next couple of days.

The academic staff thought the School came over well and seemed to be thriving. That could only be a good thing for their jobs and careers.

The non-academic staff members were proud that the School was in the news and was a topic of conversation in the shops and pubs they frequented.

Only a few parents saw the report as most pupils came from outside the area. The ones that saw it dismissed it as the usual promotional guff, but wondered if fees would be going up.

The Founder seemed relaxed about it all, as he kept spouting that he had heard that all publicity was good publicity so long as they spelt your name correctly.

The HOG was not in the least bit worried, saying that nobody of any importance read the local paper anyway.

The Headmaster was pleased the photos had come out well. To anyone who asked or commented, he said that he had been misquoted at every turn and was appalled at the low standard of local journalism

Nobody seemed concerned, apart from the Bursar, that it showed the Headmaster to be rather a loose cannon with a significantly different view of the direction the School should be taking than had been held before.

'Who can control him now? Thank God I'm retiring,' he said to himself as he quietly photocopied the article three times and sent one each to the School Solicitor, the Old Matron and the GWH.

The relevant pages were used as wrapping paper a week or so later by a young man who had a part-time job in the local fish and chip shop. He stopped mid-process.

'Look at this! He's that bloke who comes in sometimes, buys loads of portions of chips and gets me to take them to the coach parked outside. Cor, some of the sights I've seen on that bus,' he said to his boss, who replied with, 'Didn't realise he were a headmaster…'

25

THE GIANT DISCO BALL SLOWLY revolved high above the hall where the buffet supper for the Summer Ball was being served. As it was turning and turning, each tiny section of the glitter ball reflected one table at a time of the seated diners.

The circular tables were ranged around an area that had been cleared for dancing and were set out in cabaret style – each sumptuously decorated by the art department with pupil participation. Rather fetching they looked too, with added giant greenery arranged round the walls and pillars, courtesy of the grounds staff.

Over there was the table with the PTA mothers and their partners. Strange how the PTA was female-dominated and continued to be so in spite of the new Headmaster trying to draft in a few fathers.

On this occasion, as was the custom for them, the male partners were enduring the event, whereas the women, as was *their* custom, were throwing themselves into it, almost as if the whole evening had been laid on to thank them for their sterling efforts on the School's behalf over the past five years.

Constant shrieks – in an 'aren't-we-a-fun-popular-table-having-the-best-time-ever' manner – erupted every so often from this group, drawing glances of pity from the other guests.

The Headmaster's table had the HOG and his favourite journalist plus the guest speaker, a past president of the County Rugby Union Committee, the current matron and her latest beau ('Rather young, isn't he, but good luck to her!' as the PTA mothers quipped).

The other guests at the 'top table', as the Headmaster called it, were the deputy head of a feeder school and his rather charmless wife, and the School's part-time cricket coach and his wife, who was a doctor with a local practice and probably knew too much about too many of the guests for her, and their, comfort.

The Founder's table featured members of his family plus the Bursar and his wife, who was pleased to have a night out at the School's expense, having had so many nights at home ruined by her husband bringing work home with him. The Old Matron and the GWH, together with the School Solicitor and his wife, completed the table.

Actually, it was quite a jolly evening. The Founder thought it was well up to scratch and the drinks on the lawn in front of the house had been blessed by a warm and balmy evening. The harpist was a good touch, he thought. Much better than the 1960s tribute band they now had to endure. Still, it made conversation more difficult and that was not a bad thing at all as far as he was concerned. Everyone thought he was deaf anyway, so he may as well play along with that.

It gave him time, as he looked around his table and the room, to ponder how things stood with him and, more importantly, for the School. He had to admit the day had gone well. The earlier cricket, soccer and rugger fixtures of Parents and Staff v. Pupils Past and Present had been tremendous fun and terribly well supported with only a few broken limbs this year!

Everyone had enjoyed themselves immensely and the match tea afterwards was really buzzing. The new Headmaster certainly seemed popular with parents and pupils; that had been very clear. They were all taken, as the Founder himself was, by the Headmaster's physiotherapy skills on the touchline. He had seemed to be on hand wherever there was a bruise or a muscle that needed a rub down; shirtsleeves rolled up and rushing around like a proper sports medic, he cut quite a dash round the fields of play.

The Founder thought too that the Headmaster's speech had gone well, out on the terrace during drinks. It had hit just the right note, paying tribute to the founding of the School, its ethos and his determination to take it forward into the future.

His kind words were much appreciated and had prompted the Founder to sit and remember fondly those early struggles with burst pipes when the School had been cut off that first winter and seventeen boarders had huddled in their dorm with overcoats on their beds as extra blanketing.

It was, he felt, exactly the right time to hand over the reins. It had come not a moment too soon. Cometh the hour, cometh the man, he thought. I'm for the peaceful life. Time to think about myself for once.

PART TWO

26

THE HEADMASTER SAT ON THE team bus and thought about all the happy times he had spent travelling back from away matches: the camaraderie, the jokes, the games, the songs and the sweaty, fuggy air.

He was sitting with one of the boys, halfway back in the coach, as that was where he had always sat, right from the time when he himself was picked for his very first prep-school team. It was the B team actually, which explained why he had not been allowed 'up the back' with the A-team favourites of the ex-rugby league star who was their games master.

What a strange chap he had been! Welsh, six foot six and massively built, he had 'gone North' from rugby union in Wales to rugby league in Lancashire to take the money.

'I wasn't like the public school toffs of English rugby who could afford to be amateurs living off parental hand-outs and fake jobs as estate agents,' he used to say by way of justification for a life spent not playing for Wales.

The Headmaster thought at that moment, as he had not way back then, that it was ironic that this tower of terror had ended up teaching at a public school. No wonder he took it out on his pupils.

This half a Welsh mountain with coal-black hair ran the teams through fear. When he said run, you ran. When he said tackle, you tackled. It was during the very first PE lesson that he had set the tone. He had made them all line up and take their shorts off to prove they hadn't kept their pants on 'like sissies'; those who had were given the slipper – six whacks on the backside with an old plimsoll.

Still, the Headmaster had kept using the mantra that the giant forward had chanted to them before each game: 'Low tackling, straight passing, high kicking!'

In fact, he had used it at that day's game and all the boys had joined in as soon as he started with the 'Low ...'

That's something else they'd be taking with them through their lives, he thought. Tradition. That's what it means.

And the liniment! That was another tradition. He had had to use it a few times that afternoon and would need to review the injured players later to see if further applications were required.

Yet another tradition was the singing of the, to some, rather rude rugby songs like *All the Nice Girls Love a Candle*, *The Good Ship Venus*, *Eskimo Nell* and *Why Was He Born So Beautiful?* But if people thought the songs rude, they should see the First XV's initiation ceremony!

It had been a great idea of the HOG's to make up some sheets of the best-loved rugby songs to keep them alive. The boys were singing them now at the tops of their voices, helped a bit by the illicit bottles of beer that the HOG had provided and which the Headmaster was happy to turn a blind eye to.

He joined in, once more, with feeling:

If I were the marrying kind
Which thank the Lord, I'm not sir!

The Headmaster later reflected that the Summer Tour to South Africa had gone exceedingly well. Thank goodness he had a wealthy bunch of sixth-formers this year whose parents were happy to cough up a small fortune to send their golden boys on a 'life-changing trip'. Just as well that what happens on tour, stays on tour. That's what he had told them on the flight home.

The squad thought they were good players and they had bonded on the tour, but he had sensed that not all of them were quite on his wavelength. He would have to watch that. It would have to be addressed with some individual sessions of one-to-one personal coaching.

Night was falling and, by the dim lights of the coach, other traditions were being kept alive and old rituals were being observed on the final leg of the journey back to the School.

The coach journey had been a long one. The driver parked by the main gate and they all shuffled off the bus and back into the School.

'Who's for a rub down?' the Headmaster asked the team members who were all standing around in the main entrance hall clutching their kit bags, ready to head off to their dorms.

27

THE SCHOOL SECRETARY BROUGHT THE day's post into the Bursar's office along with a 'nice cup of tea' (still no biscuit).

'Looks like the usual boring brown envelopes, Bursar!'

She put the pile onto his desk along with the tea and left. He couldn't really bring himself to open it all, but as the Founder was on his way in to see him 'for a chat', he thought he had better get it out of the way.

Flicking through them, he could see that, yes, they were mostly statements from suppliers. One caught his eye, though, as it had a curious stamp on it. 'Bermuda?' he said out loud.

Dear Bursar,

It is with deep regret that we write to complain in the strongest terms about repeated incidents of bullying by members of the rugby elite of our son and others.

I am writing on behalf of the parents listed below to ask that this matter is investigated immediately and thoroughly by someone other than the Headmaster, as he would appear to be overly protective of the rugby team members, who are able to operate with impunity throughout the school in making their victims' lives a complete misery.

Complaints to members of staff have not been dealt with satisfactorily to date and the problems are ongoing.

This is the reason for writing to you directly.

Attached you will find a list of the victims with a list of the bullies and the incidents of bullying that we know about. You will note that the mildest one is where a boy's head was Sellotaped to a tree in the grounds of the School and this was actually witnessed by one of our parents.

Please inform me, by return, of the steps you intend to take.

Yours faithfully,

'Bloody hell!' The Bursar tossed the letter down and stood up, muttering, 'Why involve me, for God's sake?'

There was a knock on the door. It opened before he could even shout 'come in' and there was the Founder, clearly all dressed up and nowhere to go. Except to pop in and see his old friend.

'No need to stand, Bursar. At ease, man!'

'Actually, I think we should both sit down for this,' he replied, passing the opened letter to his visitor and motioning for him to sit.

The Founder sat down opposite the Bursar, ceremoniously took his reading glasses out of the top pocket of his tweed suit jacket and ostentatiously put them on.

He read the letter s-l-o-w-l-y and then looked up. Never show how horrified you are or display any shock when given bad news, he thought, as he remembered what his old commanding officer had drummed into him. Good advice that he had always followed.

'Put it in the master file,' he instructed the Bursar. It was their code for putting it in the bin. 'We've had all this before. Precious junior is homesick and bleats to his parents who reassure him that they will take action. They ring round a few of the other parents who they can rely on to give them sympathy and try to rally some support for their cause. They then write a stiff letter – on cardboard! – to us. Makes them feel better. Gets it off their chest and onto our desks; end of their problem, start of ours!'

'Well, this isn't the first time I've heard about this rugby stuff. I've overheard some of the staff saying much the same.'

‘It’s all poppycock! We’ve heard it all before. Every school gets it from time to time. Tell ’em you’ve looked into it, followed it up with the Board, and the Headmaster has been instructed to take the appropriate action under the School’s Code of Conduct and School Rules Policy. And by the way, you can send them a copy of the latest version. It looks pretty professional to me. The Headmaster drew it up himself after all, based on the previous one done by the School Solicitor.’

‘But isn’t that the point, sir? Shouldn’t we take an independent look at this?’

‘You’re panicking. I’m telling you to do what we did on previous occasions. It’s worked in the past. Nip it in the bud. You can’t show fear here!’

‘Look, we did it before and got away with it. But things haven’t changed, that’s all I’m saying.’

‘This mother gets it in the ear from the whining son. The father gets it in the ear from his moaning wife. Just reassure them that you have the matter in hand. All that these parents want is not to be worried at long range. They couldn’t care less about the distance that separates them from their child, but what they don’t want is for any worry to make the journey to them. Do as I say and put it to bed. The chap who has written this letter lives in Bermuda after all, so he’s not going to turn up at the School gates any time soon. Let’s give him peace of mind that we are on the case.’

‘You mean, not actually do anything?’

‘Of course I’m not saying that. Tell the Headmaster about the letter, tell him what you’ve told the parents, and tell him to sort out the boys.’

‘I can’t do that. He’ll bite my head off and tell me to leave the running of the School to him – and then *he’ll* do nothing. We can’t have that any more. OK, I’ll write to the parents along the lines you suggest, but you’ll have to speak to the Headmaster. At least he’ll listen to you. He’s got to do something, but at the same time not make it worse for the boys of these parents into the bargain.’

The Founder sighed a long, puffed-out breath of fed-upness.

‘Ohh. All right then. I’ll tell him what’s happened and what we’ve done to placate the parents and get him to rein in the rugger lot. He can report what he’s done back to you.’

The Founder forgot about the reason for his visit, which was to discuss the Bursar’s retirement party, and he forgot too about his cup of coffee – with a biscuit.

28

When the Founder left, the Bursar assumed he had gone to see the Headmaster, but noticed that he hadn't even taken the letter with him. He assumed, therefore, that all the Headmaster would get is a short lecture recommending that he tells the rugby seniors to curb their horseplay for a while and avoid contact with the boys further down the School.

Still, the list didn't just read like instances where high jinks had got out of hand. What if this was merely the tip of the iceberg?

He walked over to his bookcase, took out the latest copy of the School Rules and re-read the Anti-Bullying Policy. It was a comfort read for parents. It was a supportive read for pupils. It was clear enough about bullying being

WRONG. It gave the avenues to seek help: from teachers, the matron, the School doctor, or even the vicar of the School church, for heaven's sake.

It didn't say what to do if the School then did nothing. The section on how the School was supposed to deal with bullying could not be clearer; ACTION would be taken IMMEDIATELY and disciplinary steps set in motion, ending in expulsion for a persistent bully.

The Rules clearly stated that a formal complaint should go to the master-in-charge of pastoral matters. Then why have they written to me? he thought.

He wondered whether the School had received complaint letters in the past and had ignored them. Nothing had ever been raised in any management meetings. Surely the staff must know what's going on?

The Bursar wondered whether the whole place had turned a blind eye to all this.

His retirement could not come soon enough.

29

THE FOUNDER HAD GONE STRAIGHT to the Headmaster's study and, finding him in, had breezed in trying to make light of the morning's letter of complaint.

'Ah, Headmaster! I'm glad I've caught you. We've had another of those nasty complaint letters. For some reason it went to the Bursar of all people and not to our pastoral chappy.'

'Why hasn't the Bursar brought it to me instead of worrying you about it?'

'I popped in to see him, actually, to try and discuss his leaving do. He'd just read the letter so he shared its contents with me, unfortunately. I'm sure he would have brought it to you otherwise.'

‘Don’t be too sure. He seems to think he should be running the School.’

‘Oh, I very much doubt that. He’s always been happy to be second-in-command.’

‘Well, where’s the letter?’

‘Don’t worry about that. It’s the usual stuff. The rugby boys are lording it over the younger boys so that had better stop. You should tell them that we’ve received serious letters of complaint and that any further bullying will have consequences.’

‘Very well. I’ll put the whole first team down for extra training and tell them it’s cold showers for a week. See if that calms them down. It’ll certainly help the team’s performance. The trouble is, I can’t stop youthful high spirits all of the time.’

‘Yes, but you can keep them out of the lower school dorms and tell them the woods are out of bounds for a month. Why not?’

‘OK. OK.’

With that, the Founder left the Headmaster who looked up and around his room for a moment or two, tut-tutted and resumed writing out the First XV team for the upcoming Saturday’s grudge match against the local comp.

30

THE FOUNDER LEFT THE SCHOOL AND, after a rather wistful look at the autumnal wisteria that, despite the season, still covered the stone building to good effect, he went to his car and decided to drive into town for a coffee.

He felt shell-shocked, in reality, despite his breezy confidence and the bold sweep-it-under-the-carpet advice he had dispensed to the Bursar and the Headmaster.

This was when he missed the Old Headmaster, who had always dealt with this sort of problem in the past. But even he had had his concerns, hadn't he, about the swagger of the rugby boys and his Deputy Head?

What was the phrase he had used to describe them? 'They're like some kind of Praetorian Guard,' he would say.

Towards the end he had said at one point: 'I can see I'll have to watch out for this upstart Caesar with his own fifth column!'

Why had he said that? Had he had complaints that weren't dealt with?

Over his coffee, the Founder had tried to read his newspaper, but stopped at the Obituaries page and, seeing a few names he recognised, shivered at the latest turn of events that had beset him. It all gave him a racing heart and an overwhelming feeling of anxiety.

What next with that ruddy School, he thought. Will I ever be shot of it?

He tried to gather himself. Let's get back to first principles. How would the army have dealt with this in the old days? An ear-wigging from the CO? Or a court-martial for the offending officer, perhaps?

Either way, it would have been a private affair. No parents. No press. Just establish the pertinent facts and take decisive action with no detailed explanation needed.

All this open accountability claptrap stifled swift action. Even if the School wanted, informally, to encourage the Headmaster to move on, he would probably sue them for unfair dismissal. And win! Of course he wouldn't volunteer to walk the plank; he would merely bluster it out as he'd presumably done before. What a waste of time it all is!

But the Founder knew that this was not something he could wish away. He would have to go back and see the Bursar and review all the options with him.

He paid his bill and left the cafe, completely unrefreshed. Returning to his car, he headed back to the School.

Round two, he thought to himself as he drove. A three-line whip to close ranks and hush this up. That was still the best way forward, surely to God?

31

MEANWHILE, THE BURSAR HAD IMMEDIATELY written off, as instructed, to the complaining parent, but had done so with severe misgivings. It was no good. He knew he would have to tackle the Founder again about all this.

Some sort of internal investigation was called for, surely?

Who knows what, I wonder? Were other teachers covering this up? Is there a conspiracy of silence here? Is fear a factor? Should I consult with the School Solicitor? Perhaps he knew what had happened in the past? What did the Old Matron know? Was there anything at all in the current pupil files? What about archived pupil files?

One thing's for sure. I must get this letter and its attachments copied and get a file started. I'm not going to bin this. This time, I'm not going to cover anyone else's backside but my own!

32

THE FOUNDER WAS SOON DRIVING up the long drive on his way back to the School. Each time he did this drive he felt that it was with a heavier and heavier heart.

The sports fields looked immaculate, but even so were still being worked on, and he tried to concentrate his mind on all the good things the School had done for its pupils through the years.

People believed in the place and what it could do for their children. They had put their trust in it and had faith in the care and education that it would provide. The children themselves had, by and large, thrown themselves into it and they were a happy lot, weren't they?

All this could be wiped out by a few messy incidents unless they were very careful. Was it worth sacrificing those hundreds of satisfied customers whose high opinion of the School and their own self-worth would be destroyed?

Reputation was everything: for the survival of the School, for the pride of the pupils, and for the contentment of the parents.

Surely in some way, the moral profit and loss account had enough credits in it to still be ahead of the debits created by this new Headmaster?

After all, he mused, headmasters come and go. It was the institution that remained. But only if its reputation was safeguarded.

As if in a trance and with these thoughts in mind, the Founder returned to the Bursar's office just before lunchtime.

33

IT WAS A GLORIOUS INDIAN summer's day and the Bursar had decided, after lunch, to go for a short walk in the grounds to clear his head and try and think what to do next.

There was a delicious smell of new-mown, slightly damp, dew-wet grass and the grounds staff were clearly doing a very good and thorough job of preparing for the weekend's sporting fixtures.

He exchanged waves with the head groundsman on his tractor and set about contemplating how on earth he should proceed.

The lunch had been without incident, unless you counted the very fixed icy glare that the Headmaster had given him from where he sat surrounded by members of the rugby team.

The Bursar knew how delicate a school's reputation was, but he felt that he really had to do something and it was becoming increasingly obvious that he would be acting on his own.

The Founder had returned to the School just before lunch and had cornered the Bursar again in his office. The Founder still felt that this was an issue that should be kept under wraps, that he and the Bursar should interview the Headmaster to find out what, and what-the-hell-else for that matter, had been going on.

The Bursar had put in a spirited defence that they should look at all the evidence that might be in the pupils' files, past and present, and also interview key members of staff, past and present, to try and establish as many facts as possible so that they could decide how to proceed and what action to take.

The Founder had exploded at this with, 'Over my dead body! We must preserve the reputation of the School at all costs. It's too important. It's more important than the welfare of a few sensitive souls. It's all right for you. You're retiring. You've got your pension. You don't care that the School could be ruined by all this. Think of the pupils past and present as you keep saying – it will be their lives blighted too by their association with a tarnished school.'

The Bursar shuddered at the recollection of this outburst and was momentarily comforted by the sound of birdsong from the trees to one side of him and the gentle machine noise of the grass being cut on his other side.

He resolved to telephone the School Solicitor, in confidence, to ask him for a meeting and get his advice so that they could review the different options and agree tactics for the best way to proceed.

34

It emerged from his conversation with the School Solicitor that there had been a couple of incidents that the Old Headmaster had consulted him about and, as now, that had been in confidence.

These incidents had largely been buried because the member of staff who had raised the various concerns had been unwilling to take matters further, saying that he would refuse to take part in any investigation and, what's more, that he was taking up a teaching post at an international school in Spain and so would be out of the equation. He had assumed that once he had reported it, the issue would be dealt with by the School.

The School Solicitor had said that he remembered one of the reported incidents being that the teacher concerned had seen the Deputy Head (as he then was) sitting on a sofa with his arm around a boy. Another incident had been witnessed on a rugby trip where younger boys were forcibly held down and given love bites without the supervising members of staff taking any action whatsoever.

At the time, recalled the School Solicitor, the Old Headmaster had assured him that the matter had been investigated, but had been difficult to take any further through lack of corroborative evidence and a refusal of any of those involved to co-operate.

The School Solicitor said that he felt that it might be useful to talk to this chap again if he could track him down. He would therefore do his best to get hold of him as he thought that he still had the fellow's parents' telephone number somewhere.

The Bursar and the School Solicitor arranged a meeting for the following morning at eleven a.m., at which the letter and its attachments could be reviewed and a course of action agreed.

35

THE FOLLOWING MORNING THE BURSAR began losing his nerve and at nine o'clock, the earliest he felt he could ring, he called the School Solicitor and said that perhaps he was making a mountain out of a molehill after all and they should let the Founder and the Headmaster deal with it.

He was retiring soon and his job role did not include the pastoral or academic side. He was exceeding his brief by getting involved and was way out of his area of expertise.

The School Solicitor had been calming, but he had said that the cat was out of the bag, so to speak. The Headmaster was the common denominator in all this.

They had a duty of care to pursue it and the letter of complaint that the Bursar had received had to be taken seriously.

At this stage, the School Solicitor pointed out, the Bursar did not know what further action the parents might contemplate.

The School could not afford to be wrong-footed. It had to take the initiative otherwise it would play very badly if it all came out in the future that they had ignored serious allegations brought to their attention.

The Bursar cursed himself for being too eager to seek further 'outside' advice, but knew that all this was right and proper.

And so it was that shortly after eleven o'clock, the School Solicitor had the letter and its attachments in front of him and had read them most intently.

'First of all, this is very worrying. Analysing the letter and the attachments, it's clear that there are some direct allegations with evidence from the boys concerned, whilst other allegations are based on hearsay only, alleging activities which are supposed to have taken place on rugby trips, in dorms or elsewhere on School property.'

'Can we ignore the ones which took place elsewhere then?'

'No, I'm afraid not.'

'Well. What do you make of it?'

'I have to say that this makes very unsavoury and unpleasant reading. I cannot believe the Founder has not realised that there are now some formal stages that we must go through.'

'He can't seem to get over the fact that the School's reputation could be ruined. Twenty years ago he would have taken this on and, at best, sent the Headmaster on his way with a reference and, at worst, but only if absolutely necessary, would have frog-marched him off the premises and hang the consequences. But now...'

'That's a familiar problem. He has no real executive role here anymore, doesn't have the appetite for a long, drawn-out battle and thinks opting for the easy way out will see the problem disappear. That simply won't happen.'

'Why not? Why can't we make it disappear?'

'Well, for a start, we'll have to report this as soon as possible to the various responsible agencies: the child protection team of the local social services, the Department for Education and, by the looks of it, the police.'

'Jesus. Is that all necessary straight away?'

'I'm afraid so. Doing so protects the School or it could face even more drastic measures.'

'I can't take all this in. Yesterday morning I received a disturbing letter. Today I'm responsible for unleashing the dogs of war. What have I started?'

'You haven't started anything. You've taken the only course of action open to you. You and I are morally and professionally honour-bound to do the right thing. I suggest you now leave this to me. I'll have a word with social services and we'll take it from there. They'll have procedures to set in place.'

‘What on earth should I do about telling the Founder? And what the hell do I do about the Headmaster?’

‘I suggest we telephone the Founder now, but we mustn’t say anything to the Headmaster until social services have told us how to play this.’

36

The Founder was, unfortunately for him, at home when the phone rang and he found himself on a conference call with the School Solicitor and the Bursar.

'We're calling to discuss the next step in relation to the complaint letter you received yesterday,' the School Solicitor said by way of introduction.

'Sorry, but why are you involved? We haven't instructed you to act for us in this matter, have we?'

'I'm afraid that's my doing,' said a nervous Bursar.

'Well, bloody well undo it, man!' came the reply. 'This isn't a health and safety issue.'

'I'm afraid health and safety are the least of the School's worries.'

'Look, I'm unhappy about this meeting you're having happening at all and certainly without the Headmaster. I think you'll have to abandon it until I can be there. What's more, you haven't been instructed to act in this matter, so it doesn't concern you.'

'Well I'm here, not just as School Solicitor, but as a director. So that answers that point. But the other thing is that the Headmaster can't be in on things at this stage as he is a prime suspect in all this.'

'Suspect? What are you talking about? You don't know what you're talking about! This is nonsense. This is a School disciplinary affair and you must let us deal with it in our way.'

'That's just it though. It can't be dealt with internally. The breaches of the child protection system and laws are evident and will have to be reported and then investigated. The Headmaster will probably be suspended.'

'This is a disaster. I don't want you representing the School. I've been thinking for some time that we need a new solicitor. *I* need a new solicitor. You will not act for me or the School.'

'Steady on, sir, if I may interject. Don't be rash. Particularly at this, our hour of need, as it were. We need a calm head and some sound advice.'

'Bursar! You've done enough damage. I don't need you telling me what to do. You've done more than enough already.'

‘Let’s all stay calm here. I suggest we meet tomorrow. Whether you like it or not, the Bursar and I will be reporting this to the relevant authorities in the morning. The Bursar will be noting all this down so that we can keep a proper record from now on of our discussions and actions. Delays will count against us and might lead to dreadfully punitive action against the School.’

‘Hang on. I haven’t said all that,’ claimed the Bursar.

‘Now see what you’ve done. I’ll see you tomorrow at nine a.m. sharp,’ came the rejoinder.

The conference call ended.

37

'It's all moving too fast for me,' said the Bursar to the School Solicitor when the call ended.

'That's what happens in cases like this, I'm afraid. And it's the way it has to be. Once we've reported it, we'll have a team here within twenty-four hours to take the lead.'

'I'm beginning to regret what I've done. I'm not sure what I think anymore. Perhaps we should have had it out with the Headmaster and rooted out the cause of all this, given him his marching orders, recruited a new head and started a new, better regime.'

'It wouldn't have happened like that.'

'And I feel responsible for you losing the School as a client, as well as the Founder.'

‘That’s been on the cards for a while, ever since the Old Headmaster died. I’m too associated with the old regime. The Founder’s body language has given his feelings away before and, as for the Headmaster, well, he has always seemed to mistrust me, almost as much I do him.’

‘I think that the Founder has never been keen on washing the School’s dirty linen in public, that’s all.’

‘Well, the problem really is that he hasn’t made sure it was being washed in private either. That’s why this is happening. And that was the problem in the Old Headmaster’s time.’

38

THE NEXT MORNING, THE FOUNDER and the Bursar sat on opposite sides of the large mahogany desk in the Bursar's office. They made a prickly pair!

The Bursar had offered his resignation, but that had been refused as an empty gesture.

'No, no, no! You don't get out of it that easily. You've got to see this through. You started it and you'll finish it too.'

'But I've only been doing what I thought was right for the School, to secure its future.'

'Let's not start all that again. Let's see what our legal eagle has got to say and try and salvage things.'

There was a knock on the door and in walked the School Solicitor, briefcase in hand. After cursory hellos, they all took their seats and the Founder sought to take the lead.

'My views on this are well known to you both, so I won't rehearse them now. I want to start by saying that a person is innocent until proven guilty in my view and I'm sure that there are perfectly reasonable explanations for what has gone on. Most of it is no different from what goes on in any private school where boys are cooped up together. All schools, and rugby teams and clubs up and down the country for that matter, would recognise that we are no different from their own experiences. You might just as well investigate every school and sports club in the country. You'd find they're all the same. That's why I want to handle it internally and put it right.'

'That sounds to me like you'd rather we were keeping a lid on it,' said the School Solicitor.

'Well, yes. That's about the size of it, I suppose. What's wrong with that?'

'Well, I think we should review what we've got so far. I've made a summary which you should read.' He opened his briefcase and drew out a folder containing a number of printed pages, which he handed out to the other two. 'I've managed to turn up an old file that I thought had been turfed out a few years ago. It contained a rather interesting letter written by the Old Headmaster, which bears the legend,' he holds up the letter and reads from the envelope, '"To be opened only after my death with witnesses present, should this file be referred to again".'

'What file? What the devil is this?' The Bursar sat forward.

'It's a file about a complaint against the then Deputy Head. You will recall me telling you, Bursar, that there had been a case a few years back where a teacher had brought certain matters to the Old Headmaster's attention, but then refused to substantiate them. It would appear from notes in the file that the Old Headmaster had done a bit of a follow-up investigation. Perhaps the letter contains more about what he discovered.'

'This is getting rather ridiculous,' huffed the Founder. 'We're dealing with the here and now. This letter should be ignored in my opinion. It can't be treated as evidence without the Old Headmaster here to explain it. I don't think it should even be read. What do you think, Bursar?'

'I think we should certainly start with what we know with the complaint letter and its attachments and perhaps you could take us through this summary sheet you have so kindly prepared,' he said, looking leadingly at the School Solicitor.

'Right you are. Let's look at my summary of the allegations:

- *Pupil A – forced to swallow a condom and then given a painful wedging.*

- *This boy's father, on a visit to the School, witnessed a boy Sellotaping another boy's head to a tree and, on another occasion, observed attempts to push a boy out of a window.*
- *Pupil A and others – regular bullying by boys who were part of an inner circle of rugby players. Younger boys forced into acts of intimacy for amusement.*
- *Reports from other parents – the debagging of players on rugby tours with the boys concerned forced to hobble the length of the coach and sit next to a teacher. An initiation ceremony at which the Headmaster would 'measure up' a boy and announce the results to the coach to general amusement.*
- *Reports of players being selected as 'man of the match' and made to sit naked next to the Headmaster.*
- *Pupil A and others – nocturnal visits by senior boys to the dorms of the younger boys to engage in acts of a sexual nature.*
- *Pupil B – reports that he was seen practising a speech on the School stage whilst naked in front of the Headmaster.*
- *Pupil C – forcibly held down with other younger boys whilst older boys administered love bites to their chest, neck and buttocks. These bites left bruises and sores on the boys' bodies and were extremely frightening events.*

'I think you'll agree, gentlemen, that this makes grim reading.'

'Yes, but how do we know any of it is true? These pupils might be fantasists.'

'We have a duty of care and witnesses must be treated fairly and assumed to be speaking truthfully. That's why we must report this matter at once to social services, so that the facts can be established by outside agencies to test their authenticity.'

'So that's it, is it?'

'Well, not quite. There is this letter from the Old Headmaster. I think we should open it and read it.'

'Oh very well then. Let's get it over with.'

The School Solicitor opened the letter and read:

TO WHOM IT MAY CONCERN

Certain matters have come to my attention concerning the past and present behaviour of my current Deputy Head.

That he remains in post at the time of writing this letter bears testament to the fact that I have not been able to establish 'beyond reasonable doubt' that the alleged activities took place.

My informant wished to be anonymous, refused to substantiate his allegations – certainly to third parties – and has left the School.

Naturally, I challenged the Deputy Head who strenuously denied all the allegations.

His defence was twofold:

1. *The events 'never took place' and the pupils involved 'would deny them'.*
2. *The informant was motivated by 'spiteful vindictiveness' as he had never got over the fact that he had not been appointed as deputy head himself.*

It would appear, after I had challenged a sample of two pupils and two members of staff, that both of these defences held water.
Nevertheless, I am sufficiently troubled by what I have heard that I feel I must record the allegations – see attached list.

'You will see from the list that they pretty much replicate the current crop of allegations.'

The School Solicitor resumed his reading of the letter:
It is clear that, as you are reading this letter, further problems have been encountered and a pattern of behaviour may now be found to exist. Further investigations should be undertaken if the accuser or accusers can be persuaded to assist in those investigations.

Be advised that the Deputy Head's reaction also included a threat not only to sue the informant if he persisted in making such defamatory allegations, but also to report the matter to the Union and to take action against the School.

The School Solicitor broke off. 'What do you make of that?'

The Founder was first to respond. 'That's exactly what I mean. An enquiry was discreetly held and, when it was found to amount to nothing, no harm done to the School or to the man's career.'

'That's not the reaction I expected. Nor is it worthy of you. What do you think, Bursar?'

'Careful what you say, man,' the Founder warned him.

'Well, I assume this refers to the time the Old Headmaster consulted you. How convinced was he over the allegations?'

The School Solicitor paused before replying. 'He was in a quandary. He had asked two members of staff who had been around for quite a while and he had had a general chat with a couple of senior boys. He got nowhere, so decided to draw a line under it. At that point there were no clear-cut allegations and the accuser was an unreliable and reluctant witness.

'His conclusion was that it was mainly about the then Deputy Head's rugby boys and their activities being out of control. There was nothing about any particular child and nothing *from* a child about suffering ill treatment. Having nothing specific to go on, he felt he could hardly inform the authorities at that stage. Perhaps he should have gone further into it.'

‘There you go again,’ said the Founder. ‘You want to dredge all the time. If you dig deep enough, you’ll find something, that’s for sure.’

The School Solicitor stood up at this point.

‘Gentlemen. Our path is clear. We now have incidents that we’ve been informed about where there are allegations of improper behaviour by the Headmaster as well as other related goings-on. We have this historical file note pointing to a potential situation that the problems stretch back over many years. We have a legal obligation to inform the authorities and the School should do this swiftly. If we don’t, we’ll be acting unlawfully and that could have dire consequences. We need to be united in the decision to take this action. Bursar, do you agree?’

‘Yes.’

‘Can we count on your support as Founder and Chairman of the Board?’

‘We’re being railroaded into this. I don’t agree with it, but I can’t stop it. You two will have to handle it day-to-day and, as the saying goes, when the shit hits the fan you’ll have to pick up the pieces.’

The School Solicitor sat down again. ‘Thank you. I’ll call social services tomorrow morning and let you know what they propose. In the meantime, not a word to anyone. Repeat anyone. And that includes our pastoral bod, as well as, of course, the Headmaster himself. I suggest you call a Board meeting in the next few days as there will be a lot to discuss and follow-up action to agree.'

The Bursar turned to the School Solicitor. 'Oh God! What do we tell the parents?'

'Nothing at the moment, until we know what's going to happen and in what order.'

PART THREE

39

THE SCHOOL SOLICITOR'S PHONE CALL to social services had met with an immediate call back, as he knew it would, and an appointment with an enquiry manager had been arranged for later that very morning for an initial briefing.

At that meeting, it was outlined that a team had already been set up (with a 'team leader', no less) who would co-ordinate the activities of the police, social services, the county inspectorate and the county council's legal department.

The team leader indicated that he would be visiting the School at the earliest opportunity and the School Solicitor told him that he would see to it that he was invited to a special Board meeting at which he could outline the steps to be taken.

Later that afternoon, with the Board meeting fixed for two days' time, the team leader shared the news in a phone call to the School Solicitor that the police already had a file on the Headmaster following allegations raised by two separate individuals, who had seen his photo in the local paper. It was looking like the first action would be to invite the Headmaster to the police station for an interview. This would trigger his suspension by the School as the enquiry got underway.

40

THE BOARD MEETING WAS A subdued affair with an undercurrent of bad feeling.

Seated around the table were the Founder, the Bursar, the Old Matron and the HOG in his role as master-in-charge of pastoral matters. Also present, and on opposite sides of the table, were the School Solicitor and the Founder's new solicitor.

Whilst they awaited the eleven o'clock arrival of the team leader from social services, the Founder started things off badly: 'This is the blackest day in the history of the School. A decision to voluntarily report ourselves to social services will now bring a process of intense scrutiny of every area of the School and all the people who work and study in it. I'm sure the Bursar and the

School Solicitor acted as they thought proper. We shall see what these actions, guided by high moral principles, will result in. I hope that the outcome is not what I fear it might be.'

'Excuse me, Mr Chairman,' responded the School Solicitor, 'but I would like it minuted that the Bursar and I have acted according to our legal obligations. Whether we are right morally, others can judge, but a school cannot act outside the law when it is responsible for its pupils and for its staff.'

'*I* would like it minuted that I feel we have overreacted and panicked,' said the Founder.

'Look, that's hardly so and the Board should await the arrival of social services to see what really is the case and what further information they might have.'

The Bursar looked solemn and red-faced and clearly had things to get off his chest. 'Can I add something here? Yesterday, I had a session with our pastoral officer who is sitting opposite me here today. He gave me a file that he had not so much compiled as merely gathered together over the past several years, into which he had put quite a few complaints about the behaviour of certain pupils and members of staff. No further action seems to have been taken in any of the cases. That's a savage indictment of the attitude that prevailed in the School. I've been ashamed to have found out all this.'

The School Solicitor agreed. 'The Bursar is right. It also appears that the police have received outside complaints about the Headmaster and have a file on him already. This is worse than we can imagine.'

The HOG looked sheepish when the Founder rounded on him and said, 'Is this true? Is there such a file?'

'Yes.'

'Why did you do nothing? And doing nothing, why didn't you destroy it?'

'I kept it as insurance if I felt things had gone too far, which I didn't think they had at the time. I spoke to the Headmaster about the complaints, but didn't note those conversations in the file.'

'Are you sure you weren't keeping them to safeguard your own position with the Headmaster?' The School Solicitor was taking up the prosecutor's role. 'I could see the file having quasi-blackmailing potential.'

'Certainly not. And I resent the implication.'

The Bursar leapt in as witness for the prosecution. 'Are you sure it didn't secure you the special pay allowance for your assistance with rugby coaching, or enable you to remain in staff accommodation even though someone in your position is not usually entitled to it?'

'Those are preposterous claims and I deny them categorically. You can prove nothing at all.'

The Old Matron looked close to tears and angry at the same time and said, in a quiet voice: 'This is not getting us anywhere. What happens next?'

As if appointed acting chairman, the School Solicitor outlined what might happen next. They would have the briefing from social services. The Headmaster would have to be seen and suspended for the duration of the enquiry, unless he resigned during it. An acting head should be named. It was probably best that parents need not be alarmed with a knee-jerk announcement, and a letter to them could wait until something meaningful could be provided as to the turn of events and the likely outcome. Social services would advise.

'One thing is for sure,' said the Founder. 'You are no longer the School Solicitor. You remain on the Board for the time being, but from now on the School's new solicitor will take over this case on our behalf. Thank you for your services to the School in the past, but I cannot bring myself to thank you for your services over this matter.'

The Bursar and the Old Matron were the only ones present who were saddened by this announcement. Both got to their feet when the School Solicitor himself stood up to take his leave with these words: 'The School will be a better place for all this. Better for the staff and the pupils, if not for the owners. I wish you well.'

With that, he gathered his papers and left the meeting room. There he met the social services representative and, after a brief hello, explained what had just happened.

'They have shot the messenger in a manner of speaking, but they have got the message, at least. They know it's very serious. It's over to you now, but you'll have to take the initiative and force things along. The Bursar is likely to be of most help to you. Good luck.'

PART FOUR

41

Events then moved quickly and largely outside the control of those who had previously held power in the School.

The enquiry, lasting several months, was full, exhaustive and exhausting to all involved. Hundreds of pupils and staff were interviewed in carefully controlled environments.

There were found to be numerous cases of bullying, sexual and physical child-on-child abuse perpetrated by successive pupils over a number of years. There were allegations of staff-on-staff physical abuse and suggestions of staff-child inappropriate behaviour.

There was found to be a culture of acceptance and a condoning attitude from persons in authority to these activities, especially the rugby-playing elite victimising juniors over a number of years.

The Headmaster was suspended and resigned a month or so later.

The social services team interviewed pupils past and present as well as staff past and present.

The police investigated allegations against the Headmaster and others. The county inspectorate, together with social services, inspected the School premises, its policies and procedures, its control and discipline, and gathered favourable and unfavourable views and comments from pupils and staff.

The School's accommodation, rules and procedures were improved considerably as a result of the reports received and the implemented changes were supervised by the enquiry team.

The Bursar had had the unenviable task of informing the parents at various stages of the developments at the School.

The first letter to parents (previous questions as to the whereabouts of the Headmaster had been fobbed off with him 'working from home on plans for the future') referred to '*the suspension of the Headmaster, whilst certain allegations are investigated*' and that the School would be '*carrying on as normal during this time*'.

The second letter dealt with the fact that staff and pupils would be interviewed '*as part of the thorough and ongoing examination of the workings of the School. Social services will be conducting the interviews in carefully controlled settings with the opportunity provided for parental involvement.'*

The third letter gave the news of the Headmaster's resignation and the appointment of the HOG as the new Acting Head. The Founder added his own message:

> ***Special message to all parents from the Founder***
> *Parents can rest assured that the School has all matters in hand and every aspect covered.*
> *The academic and sporting activities remain unaffected and morale is excellent amongst the staff and pupils. The unfortunate events are being turned to our advantage with all responding, and rising, to the challenges the School faces.*
> *I am personally available to any parent who wishes to speak to me about any matter whatsoever and you have my personal assurances that the School will go from strength to strength with the worrying times now being put behind us.*
> *The Acting Head has already demonstrated outstanding leadership qualities in these troubling circumstances and I am confident that there is now a robust environment for staff and pupils alike to flourish anew.*

42

THE BURSAR RETIRED AND WAS REPLACED.

A new headmaster was appointed from outside the School – chiefly for his sound track record in pastoral care.

The School Solicitor no longer acted for the School and he and the GWH resigned as non-exec directors. The enquiry team manager said that it was the view of those in the enquiry team that, 'It is greatly to the School's credit that concerns relating to the Headmaster and other matters came to light as a result of self-referral by the School authorities.'

The former Headmaster was jailed.

43

SOME YEARS LATER, IN A churchyard in Sussex, a few friends of a 'just buried' young man hung back from the other mourners. They had been fellow pupils at the School and had known the deceased there, but none of them had been in touch with each other, or him, in quite a while.

A light snow covered the burial ground and the whiteness, with the freshly dug mound of earth at the side, made the grave look like a piece of crumbled Christmas cake once the icing has been broken through.

The eulogy in the church had spoken of the tragic loss of one so young, who had not been able to develop his full potential and whose bouts of depression had finally taken hold and cut short a precious life.

The burial over, family and friends had been invited to a small local hotel, as is the usual practice, so that the main topic of interest might be avoided over canapés and drinks, a tactic that rarely succeeds.

The graveside lingerers made their own arrangements and agreed to go to a nearby pub.

A round of beers and a quiet corner later, the friends awkwardly started off their own post-mortem.

'Not one use of the word suicide, you notice.'

'Hardly surprising.'

'And not one mention of why he was so messed up.'

'And no representative from the School.'

'How strange!'

'I feel guilty that we didn't see it coming.'

'He hid it well. After all, he'd had plenty of practice of doing that at the School.'

'We should have done more.'

'Like what?'

'Yes, what could we have done? We all just try and blot it out, don't we.'

'Good luck with that!'

'I haven't spoken to anyone about it all since the enquiry, have you?'

'Of course not. What do you think?'

'We should meet up from time to time and help each other to come to terms with it all.'

'What good would that do? We've got to draw a line under it and move on, otherwise an early grave will take us too.'

'But we've never even told each other what happened, let alone anyone else. I haven't even told my partner.'

'Now isn't the time. We should be at the hotel, at least to pay our respects to his parents.'

'Them? We owe them nothing. Neither did he. Fat lot of use they were to him when he needed them.'

'Even so, we should go. But can we come back here after half an hour or so? I want to share something rather important with you all.'

'You can't say that and expect us to wait.'

'Yes, you'll have to tell us now. *Then* we'll go to the hotel.'

'Very well. It's just that I received a letter this morning, obviously posted just before he committed suicide. I didn't get it until after the inquest because it went to my old flat and it's only just been sent on to me. I assume I was the only one of us to get it. I don't know what to do about it. Should I show it to the parents? Should I give it to the police?'

'Never mind all that. What does it say?'

'I've got it right here. Let me read it to you all...'

I'm not sure whether this letter is necessary or not. I assume that you will have had some of the same feelings and thoughts that I have had over the years about our time at the School.

I wonder if you and any of the others have come through it better than I have? The fear I felt at the time has not gone away at all.

The lack of any support from my parents or teachers was the worst aspect of the whole situation and the most difficult to forgive.

I cannot stand to hear the noise of footsteps outside a darkened room without being taken back to that time in the dorm.

You can imagine, I'm sure, that every night, when people in the neighbouring flats return home, the thud, thud, thud of their footsteps on the stairs strikes me with terror and foreboding. Even now, I can't go to bed without fearing the worst.

I can't stand to hear the ref's whistle from the nearby playing fields without thinking of those rugby matches and the post-match horrors of the coach trip back and the offers of a rub down with that smelly liniment.

I can't stand in the shower without checking and double-checking the bathroom door is locked.

I can't stand hearing my name called out at the dentist's or doctor's surgery without thinking that the Headmaster is calling for me.

I'm completely obsessed with what happened at School and constantly relive it, wondering if we could have done more to stop it happening to us or to others.
I keep hearing one of the teachers saying to me after my interview for the enquiry, 'If you'd kept your mouth shut in the first place, we'd still have a headmaster.'
The only useful thing I ever did was to tell a lad who worked in the chip shop what went on at the School. He went to the police to tell them what he had heard and also what he himself had seen on the School rugby bus.
Now all I do is keep planning ways to exact revenge on the teachers who bullied and abused us and the teachers who covered it all up. But I end up doing nothing.
As you will learn, I am doing something about myself, but I am doing nothing about them.
That's up to you.

'It's signed off "*With love and affection, Pupil G*", which was how social services referred to him in the final report.'

'And that's it? Nothing else?'

'It brings it all back.'

'I hadn't any idea he was suffering so badly.'

'Well, don't you?'

'Not like that, no!'

'What shall I do with it?'

'Nothing!'

'What about the parents?'

'Again. Nothing!'

'What about the police and the coroner?'

'Nothing. It doesn't change anything.'

'If anything, you should send it to the School.'

'Let's talk about it after we've been to join the wake at the hotel.'

44

THE GROUP MADE THEIR WAY to the hotel, but did not stay long. They quickly bored of trying to pull the parents of their late friend down a peg or two. They were obviously grieving badly, despite trying gamely to find out how their late son's contemporaries were doing in life. It was not the place to be with the history they shared with the deceased.

After several failed attempts at insults and a few more at expressing sympathy, the group signalled to each other that it was time to leave and, after saying their farewells, adjourned to the pub.

By the time they got there, the group had become a cabal and they hatched a plot. They would be taking the request in the letter a whole lot further. Then, over a drink or two, they worked out a plan of action.

They would make contact with the police to report all those who had abused them and those who had turned a blind eye to their suffering. Out of politeness, they would also be informing the reported individuals that they were doing just that.

This would make it a much bigger investigation with more people involved than had already taken place at the School.

Maybe then, those named would gain some kind of appreciation of what they had put the boys through. They themselves would begin to fear the day or night summons to a place they had no wish to go and learn for themselves what it meant to be put through a nightmarish ordeal that they had no control over whatsoever.

45

MUCH LATER, THE FOUNDER DIED and had his own funeral at the School.

The drive was lined with a reduced number of pupils whose heads were bowed as the cortège passed. We will never know how many of them stared at the ground from obedience or from sadness at his death, or how many from the sadness that comes from the separation from parents or how many from the deep sadness, self-pity and self-loathing that comes from episodes of bullying or abuse.

What kind of film ending would that have made?

Also from Thorogood

www.thorogoodpublishing.co.uk

All Through the Night

Written in the style of an old-fashioned Western, this tale of Welsh drovers taking a large herd of cattle from North Wales to London in the 1790s, stakes a claim for these engaging characters to be considered the first 'cowboys'.

Running through this 'Welsh Western', which is rich in adventures and incidents, the storyline has the strong cultural, emotional and human elements that make Westerns so appealing in exploring how people act in the drama of their own lives.